The Unfortunate Adventures
of
Tom Hillingthwaite

The Unfortunate Adventures

of

Tom Hillingthwaite

Andy Kind

MONARCH
BOOKS

Oxford UK, and Grand Rapids, USA

Text copyright © 2015 Andy Kind
This edition copyright © 2015 Lion Hudson

Published by Monarch Books
an imprint of
Lion Hudson plc
Wilkinson House, Jordan Hill Road,
Oxford OX2 8DR, England

Email: monarch@lionhudson.com
www.lionhudson.com/monarch

ISBN 978 0 85721 432 4
e-ISBN 978 0 85721 433 1

First edition 2015

A catalogue record for this book is available from the British Library

Printed and bound in the UK, February 2015, LH26

This book is for Iain and Michelle Every.
Unashamedly.

Contents

A Note on the Text

All characters appearing in this work are fictitious. Any resemblance to real persons, living or dead, is purely coincidental.

The town of Bruton is also fictional, and is written as a large generic settlement in the South of England, or "Wessex". It is not linked to or influenced by the actual town of Bruton in Somerset.

This is not a theological or evangelistic book. It is neither primarily satirical nor allegorical. It is a story about a man.

Chapter 1

"The Name's Hillingthwaite, Tom Hillingthwaite"

The drive down from Nottingham to Bruton in Wessex had taken over three hours. As he turned the corner into the little cul-de-sac of Dews Close that was to be his new home, Tom Hillingthwaite surveyed the rest of his family – wife, daughter, two cats – and a pertinent thought struck him: he only owned one cat. Six hours later, as he once again turned the corner into the little cul-de-sac that was to be his new home (having dropped off Mr Tinkles and helped take down some of the Missing Cat posters), Tom took a moment before exiting his car to reflect on his situation.

After ten years spent rising without trace within the carpet retail industry, he had just taken up a job with Jesus4All (formerly the Turn or Burn Gospel Coalition).

If "job" is the correct term for something that pays less than the minimum wage and relies almost exclusively on the benevolence of friends and loved ones to stave off starvation, Tom mused, concluding that it probably wasn't.

Although he was effectively an evangelist, his official job title was "Community Builder". The problem with the word "evangelist" is that it's Christianese: that pseudo-language birthed in the late twentieth century by fusing biblical derivations with transatlantic management slogans, spoken by Christians in the West and understood by literally nobody else. Sensitive to this fact, the bosses at Jesus4All (formerly the Turn or Burn Gospel Coalition) were eager not to employ unhelpful terms which constructed unnecessary linguistic walls when it came to – as they put it in the job manifesto – "the business of living incarnationally and journeying with the unchurched in a missional, seeker-sensitive way whilst still leaving room for the Spirit to minister".

Tom's sense of calling to full-time ministry had led him to take an 80 per cent pay cut and leave the leafy suburbs of Robin Hood country to relocate to a place that the local tourist guide proudly referred to as "no longer the stab capital of the South-West".

"I hope you know what you're doing," Tom said, looking at the sun visor where he had attached two pictures: one of Jesus (played by Jim Caviezel), and one of George W. Bush. They were there to remind him that firstly someone had died for him, and secondly there's always someone less capable. The face looking back at him from the driver's mirror was not an unpleasant one, but neither was it one that would have won any awards – apart from one for "World's Most Generic Face". His eyes were a muddy brown, his hair miscellaneously styled. His slender nose veered to the right at its tip, while his eyebrows were slightly circumflexed so that, whatever Tom's mood, he wore a permanent look of mild bafflement. By his own admission, he was no oil painting – unless it was an oil painting undertaken by an artist totally lacking in imagination and then left out in a drizzle.

Exhausted from his nine-hour cat-ferrying service, Tom hauled himself from his knackered old red Sedan car and staggered into the squat 1950s semi in search of some TLC, R+R and other energy-replenishing monograms.

"I need you to help me move this bed-frame upstairs immediately," came the voice of his wife, Rachel. "I've smashed my leg on it three times."

"I've driven for nine hours straight, my chosen. Without food or sleep and with too many cats. I stopped for three separate wees at Tamworth Services, which I'm confident must qualify as a world record. I got so bored, I started asking Mr Tinkles for his views on penal substitutionary atonement. Please can I do it later?"

Tom didn't ask whether Rachel had considered not smashing her leg on the bed-frame three times, because he was too tired and, more significantly, because he was fasting sarcasm for Lent. Lent had actually finished the previous month, but every time he said something sarcastic, Rachel made him go back to the start. He was currently up to day three.

"Well, fine. We'll just sleep on an old mattress in the living room like a couple of squatters, shall we?" Rachel wasn't fasting sarcasm for Lent. Her face somehow balanced gentleness and authority in equal measure.

"Sounds practically salvific," said Tom, collapsing bonelessly onto the dust-sheeted mattress like a man who had driven thricely through Tamworth because of an erroneous cat.

The house being rented by the Hillingthwaites had been listed on the property website as "part-furnished", which, Tom now realised, meant that it had doors. It certainly didn't have anything else.

No, that's unfair: it has damp, thought Tom.

Indeed, an earthy and pervasive scent filled his nostrils as he lay there on the floor, half-comatose. He managed a glance at his 1988 special edition Michael Keaton Bat-watch (which was really just a fairly normal Casio with a small picture of Michael Keaton dressed as Batman on the face) and saw that it was 11:11 p.m. Tom took this as a sign of something or other, and then plummeted into a deep well of sleep.

Eight hours later, the familiar sound of his wife's voice hoisted Tom back towards full consciousness and out of an odd dream where he'd been sitting on a step crying.

"Tom? Wakey, wakey… I've made you tea and toast… although the toaster's still in one of the boxes, so it's just bread really; I held it over the hob for a bit."

Tom sat up on the mattress and got his bearings while munching on his falsely advertised toast. A sudden erratic billowing of the room's curtains caught his attention. For one horrible moment, Tom feared he was witnessing a hideous ghostly apparition, but it turned out to be his six-year-old daughter, Amy, and her cat Selina.

Standing behind the curtain, Amy squashed her face against the thin netting and announced, "Daddy, this house smells a bit like a garden. Shall we go back and live in our other house now?"

"Well… we don't have another house now, darling."

No, Daddy sold it so we could come and live in a much smaller house in a town where we don't know anyone, and that's why Daddy is sitting on a mattress eating partially heated bread. Tom didn't voice the second part of that answer, through fear that he might start sobbing openly. There are few things in life sadder than the sight of a father sitting on the floor, tears flowing down his face onto a piece of warm Hovis, like a soon-to-be-executed hostage.

"Tom, when you've finished your toast…"

"It's not toast."

"When you've finished your bread, I need you to help me move this bed-frame upstairs. I've smashed my leg on it six times."

Rachel had already been up for an hour, busying herself with tasks, her dark-chocolate hair nestled inside a large polka-dot handkerchief like a Dig-for-Britain poster-girl. Tom finished his not-breakfast, then, struggling to his feet, he emitted that first big satisfying trump of the day, sending his daughter into a fit of giggles and the cat looking around for potential predators.

* * *

Around midday, having shifted the wife-beating bed-frame, Tom decided to take a break from unloading boxes and go and introduce himself to the neighbours.

After all, I'm here to make disciples in Wessex, and the way to do that is one West Saxon at a time.

Hoping to keep things light and breezy, Tom decided to take along a china cup of fruit tea. When Rachel informed him that they hadn't yet unpacked the porcelain or the hot beverages, he ventured outside with a drink of Vimto in a small vase.

The cul-de-sac of Dews Close was little more than a recess off one of Bruton's A-roads, an uneven artexed semi-circle of squat, pug-faced buildings. The first sign of life Tom saw, as he ambled down his drive, was a middle-aged man sitting idly on a deckchair, sporting a karate outfit and holding a hedge-trimmer. Deciding to start his Great Commission there, Tom fixed his face into a simpering smile and set a short course for his new neighbour. As he got closer, Tom noticed that the one thing the man with the hedge-trimmer didn't have on his property was a hedge.

O.M.Gosh… Maybe I'll call back later when he's less busy and lethal-looking.

To his chagrin, however, Tom saw that the man had already clocked the Community Builder's beeline for him. Abruptly changing his course might look odder than a man in a karate outfit holding a hedge-trimmer. Rather than make a U-turn and retreat, Tom opted to leave the cul-de-sac entirely, nodding briskly to the man as he did so, in that very British way that is more of a nervous twitch than a greeting.

He strolled nonchalantly back into Dews Close five minutes later, long enough, he thought, to have taken in the local corner shop – something which he would have done had he not been drinking from a small vase. Instead, not wanting to look like an idiot, Tom had been standing furtively round the corner, waiting for a sensible amount of time to elapse before returning. Observing that the Kung-Fu Gardener was no longer present, he kicked the proverbial (and somewhat premature) dust off his feet, and picked a new target.

The house to the left of the Hillingthwaite residence had two cars in the drive, neither of them with the requisite number of wheels. Tom rapped on the door in a jovial way and a man in a vest opened it. He didn't look jovial, but at least he wasn't holding a hedge-trimmer.

He either has a lot of tattoos, or he's wearing a tee shirt that makes it look as if he does.

A dog was barking inside the house, and the man shouted, "Shut it, Boobies!" then locked Tom with a pair of quasi-hostile eyes.

"I think someone's stolen some of your wheels," Tom said jovially. If anything, the man now looked even less jovial than he had a few moments earlier, when he hadn't looked very jovial at all.

"Can I help you?"

Tom realised that he hadn't yet introduced himself; he might have come across as some sort of door-to-door one-liner merchant: a terrible one. The thing to do was to introduce himself suavely, like James Bond would.

"Ah, yes, sorry – the name's Tom Hillingthwaite, Hillingthwaite. I've just moved in next door. And your name is…?"

"Wayne."

"Pleased to meet you!"

"All right." There was no hint of inflection in the voice as the man said "All right". He wasn't really asking if Tom was all right.

"Is your dog really called Boobies?"

"Yeah. Kids chose the name."

Tom could see that, in addition to the post-modern Bayeux Tapestry etched on his skin, Wayne also appeared to have donated a number of his teeth in a liberal and somewhat gung-ho fashion. The dilapidated mouth sat amid a face that was bumpy and uneven, and looked like a misshapen bread roll.

There was a pause. The awkwardness was broken by two small people (children, that is, rather than dwarves) who raced past him and out into the road.

"Are those your kids, then?" Tom enquired, his joviality starting to take a thrashing.

"No, I'm a child-catcher. Those two've just escaped." The Tattooligan's four front teeth were missing and, every time he spoke, his molars and top lip formed a sort of five-a-side goal from which he fired out tiny shots of saliva.

"Oh… oh, right… really?"

Wayne looked at Tom flatly, without humour or hospitality.

"Haaa…" Tom responded, suspecting that his neighbour had never fasted sarcasm for Lent. Then, throwing in the joviality towel, he said, "Well, nice to meet you. See you around."

"Yep, see ya," Wayne the Tattooligan replied curtly, then closed the door with a sinewy mottled arm. Tom hated tattoos, and had often joked with Rachel that there was nothing scary about someone who treated their own skin like a colouring book. He now understood those words to be not just glib, but also desperately, woefully wrong: his new next door neighbour was terrifying, and was not the sort of man who treated himself like a colouring book so much as the sort of man who stuck sharp objects into his own flesh for a laugh.

"God bless you… " Tom added, quietly enough so that Wayne wouldn't hear through the door.

The house on the other side of Hillingthwaite Towers had a beautifully tended garden and a compact Nissan parked outside, sporting just the right number of wheels. After his harrowing introduction to Wayne (who was by some distance the most working-class man Tom had ever met), the scent of the garden's perfectly pruned roses acted like a dose of aromatherapy, and Tom relaxed somewhat and regained his sense of missional purpose. He knocked on the door, but nobody answered. The inhabitants were probably out, although the thought did occur to Tom that perhaps the Tattooligan had already started ringing round the neighbourhood, warning people about his cold-calling.

Dews Close contained only six houses, so Tom decided to plough on.

"Excuse me?"

From across the close a lady's shrill voice nipped at Tom's ears, and he turned to see a walking boutique high-heeling its way elegantly towards him. Her perfume introduced itself well before he saw the whites of her eyes.

"Hi there," Tom said.

"Who are you?" the lady asked with an affected pinch to her voice. She seemed slightly perturbed by his presence. Again, the thing to do was to conjure up a suave James-Bond-style introduction.

"The name's Hillingthwaite Tom. I'm the new Community Builder – just moved in."

"Oh, I see. Sorry, I thought you were spying for my ex-husband. He's not allowed within half a mile of me, so he likes to use his friends for surveillance."

"No, I'm not a spy, no."

I can't even introduce myself like one. Why did I call myself Hillingthwaite Tom? I'm not a school register.

The lady from No. 1 un-narrowed her eyes, but her overpowering fragrance was wrestling Tom's senses of smell and taste into submission.

"Community Builder, you say? Well, I hope you'll be sorting out the sewage leaks we keep getting."

"Pardon?" Tom coughed. "No, I'm not from the council. I work for a Christian charity – here to teach people more about Jes…" Tom broke off from saying the word "Jesus" to retch – a reaction usually reserved for the demon-possessed.

"Are you quite all right?" The lady seemed immune to her own olfactorily gratuitous stench.

"Yes, thank you."

"Good. So when will the sewers be corrected?"

"I'm not from the council."

"Well, tell them it's not acceptable and I want it sorted."

The lady from No. 1 tottered off on her alimony-funded heels, leaving Tom to gasp for unpolluted air. Her husband wasn't allowed within half a mile of her, but Tom suspected that he would be fragrantly asphyxiated if he even attempted it.

That perfume acts as its own restraining order.

"God loves you," he coughed meekly through a mist of *Diable pour Femmes*.

Tom made a quick journey back to his own house to refill his vase of Vimto, then resolved to press on with the (up-to-this-point-harrowing) introductions.

Endurance builds character…

The next door Tom knocked on was opened almost instantly, by a young lady in her early twenties and a nightie.

"Hello!" said Tom.

She gasped, then hid everything but her face behind the door.

"Sorry, I thought you were my boyfriend."

"I'm sorry to disappoint you… which I'm sure I would if I were your boyfriend," he offered with a candid smile. The young lady met his smile with an uncomfortable facsimile of one, and so Tom, keen to allay any fears that he might be in some way predatory, introduced himself with his standard suaveness.

"Tom Tom Hillingthwaite Tom."

"Sorry?" The young lady looked understandably confused. "Your name's Tomtom? Isn't that more of a satnav's name?"

"Yes, no, sorry, it's just Tom. My satnav's called *Dux Ducis*. My wife, daughter and I, Tom Hillingthwaite, have just moved into No. 3. I just wanted to come and introduce myself as… 'Hillingthwaite, Tom Hillingthwaite'."

Finally! Alleluia.

"Oh, right – hi, I'm Catrina," she replied, unclenching a little. "Welcome to the neighbourhood."

In the wake of his previous two confrontations, her greeting made Tom a bit emotional. He thanked her.

"So, how long have you been here, then?" he enquired. It was going quite well now, and they seemed to have left the philosophising about what would happen if Tom was her boyfriend way behind them.

"Oh, we've lived here about a year. My boyfriend just

popped out to get bacon for lunch."

"Oh, splendid – well, let me pay for that as a welcome gift." Unfathomably, Tom reached into his pocket, pulled out a £5 note and offered it to her.

Catrina began to laugh, then stopped abruptly when she realised he was serious.

"Please – let it be a blessing to you," Tom insisted.

"Erm, no, it's fine, really. We've both got jobs – we can afford bacon."

At that moment, a car pulled into the drive and Catrina's boyfriend got out in time to witness a strange man offering his girlfriend hard cash as she lurked behind the door in her nightdress.

"What's going on?" he bristled.

"Oh, hi! I was just offering to finance your meat," Tom said, leaping head first into a sea of conversational suavelessness.

"His name's Tom – he's just moved in two doors down."

"Nice to meet you, Carl!"

"Carl? My name's not Carl."

His name wasn't Carl. Tom hadn't been told his name. For some reason, the name Carl just sprang to mind and, thinking it to be a word of knowledge, he spoke it out. It wasn't a word of knowledge. It was the name Carl.

The Lord has never used the name Carl prophetically. Why would he?

Tom drained his vase of Vimto and put the £5 note back in his pocket. He bade them a good day and traipsed home, wondering whether it might already be time for another fresh start.

"Why was he drinking from a vase?" he overheard "Carl" say to Catrina.

"I think he might be a bit simple," she responded. Perhaps, Tom thought, the Lord had given her that as a word of knowledge.

"God bless you," he totally forgot to say.

"How was your time with the neighbours, honeybunny? Any more bums on seats in the Kingdom?"

Rachel extricated the vase from Tom's hand and replaced it with a screwdriver (the actual kind, not the vodka and orange juice kind – Tom had never tasted alcohol in his life).

"Well, no, not quite – I didn't really do much more than say hello."

"Well," Rachel smiled, "most relationships do start with 'Hello' – apart from ours, which started with you headbutting me."

"I was bowing to you – I didn't see you coming in for a hug."

"Who bows these days?"

"I thought we'd dealt with this, my chosen. But, you know what, you're right – you've got to start somewhere. I've only been here a few hours and already I've taken the initiative. And you can never count the profit on an order you never took."

Tom knew that was the case when it came to selling carpets, but was it applicable to spreading the Gospel in Bruton? He certainly thought so. Feeling that he'd laid some good initial foundations, he slalomed past a few boxes into the kitchen and set to making himself a couple of celebratory slices of lukewarm bread. Having first bowed to his wife.

Chapter 2

Sin City

*L*ater that afternoon, Tom was due to meet up with a couple of local church leaders. He saw it as a chance to learn more about the spiritual battleground onto which he was striding, and also to share something of his vision for the area. And to eat as many free biscuits as he could before being asked to leave.

He was a bit late leaving the house, because he had been working on his man-cave. It was becoming something of a trend among much cooler men than Tom to have a room of the house allocated solely to man stuff, with a beer fridge and a dartboard and posters of supercars. Tom had never drunk beer, threw darts like a man with a crippling case of pins and needles, and thought cars were "a wasting asset" and therefore, by definition, less than super. As a direct consequence of this fact, Tom's man-cave (which was more aptly called a garage) contained a jug of filtered water, a large collection of comics and graphic novels, and a poster of Jesus (played by Robert Powell). In terms of man-gadgets and shiny electronics, it was on a par with an actual cave; it was more of a cloister.

Tom left his man-cave, typed the postcode of the Baptist church into his satnav and headed into town. After the morning's interpersonal car-crash, he was starting to feel more positive, thanks to a couple of jars of strong mint tea ("jars" in the literal sense – they still hadn't unpacked any of the stoneware). To increase his buzz, Tom purchased a pack of cola-flavoured Chewitts from the local newsagents, then whacked *The Best of Marvin Gaye* into his in-car cassette player. If there was one thing guaranteed to warm his soul, it was a good blast of "Sexual Healing" – something he was strongly opposed to theologically, although he conceded that if that sort of healing service were on offer more regularly, every church would be full. And sweaty.

The modest research he'd undertaken into the town of Bruton led Tom to believe that it was something of a cultural and spiritual wasteland. Situated about fifty miles east of the county town of Casterbridge, a positive sign was that the evangelist Billy Graham had once graced Bruton with his presence. Less positively, so had the Black Death. The most dramatic event in recent history – in fact, since the Black Death – had been the closure of the town's public library. Its subsequent renovation into a Gentleman's Club named "The Pubic Library" had caused quite a stir in the local press (and provided helpful alibis for "confused" businessmen going there to browse). The reconstituted library now had double the members of the old place, but no Children's Section.

As he reached the far end of the High Street, *Dux Ducis* informed him that they had reached their destination. Tom glowered around but there was no church in evidence.

"Nice one, *Dux Ducis*, you idiot… Sorry, sorry, that was crass and unkind."

He parked and started scouring the area for the Baptist church. The first thing he noticed was a vandalised council-erected sign bearing the slogan: "Bruton, where the ~~magic~~ tragic happens!" Aside from bleak graffiti, the shop fronts on Bruton High Street created the slightly claustrophobic feel of too many people crammed into a lift: a long row of post-war concrete buildings with too-narrow facades, all vying for attention and air. Tom couldn't see the church. Incredibly keen not to ask for directions in the library, he accosted a man in a dog-collar heading into Boots.

If there's any social group that's going to know where the church is, it's the people in dog-collars.

"Excuse me? Do you know where the Baptist church is?"

"No, sorry," the man replied brusquely, and hurried through the automatic doors towards the pharmacy. A dainty old lady was coming the other way out of the shop.

If there's any social group that's going to know where the church is, it's the dainty old ladies.

"Excuse me…" Tom approached her with a beam. She looked startled and scuttled off like an antisocial crab.

Tom's chest cavity deflated in consternation. He was feeling like a social leper.

W.T.Flip… what's wrong with people? I don't have the Black Death – at least, I don't think so.

"Woshya problem, mate?"

Tom turned to see a wiry woman with an attractive but worry-drenched face squinting at him. She was leaning against a bollard which had been awkwardly positioned on the edge of the pavement.

"Woshya problem?" she repeated.

"Oh… I was… I'm looking for the Baptist church." He waited for a response somewhere between hostile and bodily grievous.

"No worries – just there on the end, where that crappy little red car's parked." Tom looked over towards the crappy little red car, and registered that it was *his* crappy little red car. He had parked directly outside the church and not realised it.

"Oh… thank you."

"Like I say, no worries. M'name's Vicky, yeah."

"Tom…" Tom had reneged on trying to be suave in these situations – he'd found suaveness slightly less easy than finding the Baptist church.

"Say a prayer for my boy, yeah?" Vicky asked equably.

"Suretainly will." (Speaking suavely wasn't Tom's only obstacle – sometimes, speaking words was just as much of a problem.) "What shall I pray?"

"It's his dad, yeah, so… " She tailed off and set her gaze towards something in the distance. Tom saw that the worry which drenched this young woman's face was not the sort that catches you like an unexpected downpour. It was more the sort of anxiety that drip-drips over time; that light worry that soaks you through.

"Right, well I suretain… I will definitely arrow something up for you and your lad."

She bobbed her head without making eye contact, and Tom thanked her once more and walked off towards the crappy little red Sedan and the well-hidden church.

In an ironic sense, the Baptist church stuck out on the High Street, in that it was the only building in the row that seemed not to want to draw attention to itself. The other shops along the promenade were kitted out with signage and produce, designed to beckon seductively: "Come in, friend." The church, on the other hand, seemed to whimper: "Stay away, leave us alone" – the structural equivalent of an antisocial crab.

This is not a good sign.

Tom climbed the indented stone steps, misshapen by the footfall of thousands of God-fearing soles, and heaved open the iron-clad double doors. He could have knocked, but he was already late and suffering from Bunyan bladder (that state of being so desperate for the toilet, it's akin to carrying a huge burden). As he stepped over the threshold onto the garish 1980s carpet (whose only saving grace was that it was almost entirely frayed away) he saw a woman sitting in the lobby, holding a broom.

She's either taking a break from cleaning the hall, or she's a witch engaged in some serious behind-enemy-lines spiritual warfare.

Plumping for the former, Tom offered her a greeting.

"We're closed!" she said.

"Hi, I'm Tom."

"I'm Dawn. We're still closed."

Tom changed his mind: she was definitely a witch.

"Tom Hillingthwaite – I've got a meeting to see Brian."

"Oh, right."

He limbered up his mouth to accept her apology, but it never arrived.

"Brian's out at the chemist."

"Right, so does he have an office?"

"Of course."

"Can I wait in it?"

"Locked."

"OK. Do you have a key?"

"Yes."

"Soooooo…"

With a reluctance on the scale displayed by inhabitants of the Sudetenland when welcoming division after division of mechanised Panzers, Dawn (suspected witch) rose to her feet, clumped over to the locked office, and opened it.

"Thanks very much!"

No answer.

* * *

Tom sat alone in Brian's office, gazing around idly and praying in tongues in case Dawn had put a hex on him.

It was a standard office for a member of the clergy. Stacked upon the several pregnant bookshelves were the classic staples of required ministerial reading: *The Cross of Christ, Mere Christianity, The Cost of Discipleship, Stand Up and Deliver.* Arrayed on Brian's desk was a selection of family portraits in what appeared to be chronological order: in each, Brian had considerably less hair than in the previous photo. The pictures acted as a temporal growth chart for Brian's three kids, and as a timeline of decay for the man himself.

The walls of the office had been painted with what the Dulux Colour Chart would class as "hint of excreta", and on one of these dubiously decorated walls hung a poster of a dove in front of a waterfall – one of those images that was popular for about a month in the mid/late eighties, but which still grace the walls of almost every clergy office in the UK. On closer inspection, Tom noticed that the dove had been given a handlebar moustache in black marker pen: the result of either an unattended child or a sermon-writer's mental block. On the wall to the right there was a crocheted verse hanging like a pendant. The verse said: "Be sure your sins will find you out." Tom perceived why he hadn't found any Rob Bell on the bookshelf.

Suddenly, the door opened and in trudged Revd Brian Child (an intriguing name, and one that had seen Brian wrongly credited with a lot of good ideas down the years). Tom realised that he had met Brian before – recently, in fact. He was the same minister whom Tom had accosted outside Boots and asked for help finding the church.

"Hel… oh, hi there, Tom." Brian looked embarrassed.

"Hi, Brian. I take it you did know where the church was after all?"

"Yes. I'm sorry, I thought you were wanting to break in."

"Break in? Goodness, no. Has that happened a lot, then?"

"No, not yet – but it's that sort of area." His mouth lapsed into a semi-snarl as he said the word "area".

Entering the room behind Brian was a clothed drainpipe of a man with a raspberry-ripple complexion and hair so white and unkempt that it brought to mind an exquisite meringue peak. He essentially looked like a dessert.

"Tom, this is the Reverend Dr Philip Gallowstree."

"Greetings!" replied the Revd/Doc/Delicious Pudding.

"Please, both of you, make yourselves comfortable – I'll get a brew on."

Brian filled the modest kettle in the corner of his office and brought out a scant choice of biscuits: bourbons or custard creams. This was annoying for Tom. In his entire experience of having tea with vicars, he couldn't remember ever being offered anything other than low-level biscuits like bourbons and custard creams. Tom always presumed a direct correlation between a church that only bought bourbons and custard creams and a church that had given up all hope of seeing any tangible growth. He also wondered whether, if one were to bring a packet of Italian amaretti into a British church, the world would suddenly tilt on its axis, forcing a cosmic transition shift and destroying mankind forever. Probably not, he supposed.

Good job I bought those Chewitts for the drive home.

"Do you have any fruit tea?" he asked. "I don't drink caffeine. I don't believe in artificial stimulants."

Brian looked at him and shook his head, almost disconsolately.

Revd Gallowstree piped up: "No, he doesn't, Tom… but he's got hot water and I've got a packet of Polos – will that do?" Gallowstree slapped his own thigh and bellowed with self-generated mirth.

"Just water's fine, thanks."

Brian nodded imperceptibly.

"I was interested in the crochet on the wall," Tom said to Brian, as the latter filled two cups with economy-brand teabags.

"Oh, yes. My youngest made it when she was four."

"It's nice."

"What do you mean by sin, though?" Gallowstree enquired, staring up at the crochet while trying to smooth back a particularly errant peak of meringue-like hair.

Brian's gaze fell on Gallowstree as Dagon's temple fell on Samson. Tom sensed this was not the first time they had crossed theological swords on this issue.

"What do you mean, what does he mean by sin?" Tom jumped in, unsheathing his own sword.

"What do you mean, what do I mean, what does he mean by sin?"

Gallowstree leaned back in his chair and drew his hands together in faux supplication. He was evidently gearing up for his keynote speech.

"Well, you see, we talk about 'sin' when what we really mean is human nature. Nobody's perfect, are they? And God, who created humans, knows this. What is he going to do – punish us for being humans? Balderpiffle! On the contrary, he embraces us in our human nature."

"So are you saying you don't believe in sin?" Tom asked.

"What I believe, Tom, is that all of us, Christian, Buddhist, Jedi" (he chuckled to himself) "are all trying earnestly to pursue goodness. And God, or Allah, or the Force" (he chuckled again) "rewards that. A good God doesn't – wouldn't – punish someone for trying to live a good life. The whole idea is obscene."

Gallowstree took a big slurpy sip from his cup of tea and repeatedly dunked in a bourbon, which predictably fell apart at the third dunking.

"Now, Tom, tell me why you're here," continued Gallowstree, through a mouthful of soggy biscuit.

"Well… I… erm…"

Tom felt his vocabulary dry up like an undunked ginger biscuit – apart from "suretainly", which was hanging around eagerly, ready for action when called upon. Tom had been expecting to meet up and pray with some brothers-in-arms, but Gallowstree's liberalism felt like a theological insurrection.

"I've just taken up a role on behalf of Jesus4All. I'm here as a Community Builder for Wessex."

"Excellent!" replied Gallowstree. "So many of Jesus' teachings are still relevant today, aren't they?"

"Well, I'd say all of them are." Tom was starting to think that the guy who looked like a meringue was something of a fruitcake. He decided that was quite a good joke and made a mental note to tell Rachel later.

"Yes, yes, of course, Tom, but we need to be careful not to misinterpret what he said. All this talk of hell and judgment doesn't fit with the message. Jesus was the happiest man who ever lived – we need to remember that."

"Er… Brian, what advice have you got for me?" Tom looked over at the incumbent minister, searching for an ally.

"Tom," Brian said flatly, "I've been here eight years in this God-forsaken town, and I've learned one thing above all others: evangelism doesn't work. It doesn't – I've tried it. We've done outreaches, Alpha courses, soup runs. It has no impact. People don't want to know. They've rejected the Lord, and all we can do is leave them to it."

"But don't you think–"

"Tom, I don't think any more. I just get on with it. By all means come and try to do your job, and enjoy it – but don't expect any miracles, or anything approaching that. It's a dead end."

Tom Hillingthwaite felt the colour draining from his face.

"So why do you still do the job, then?" He sounded plaintive, and he knew it.

"Well, what else am I going to do? I'm not trained for anything else. I've only got five years until I retire, so I'm just going to stick it out and then move to Llandudno. And I won't be looking back, for fear that I might turn to salt."

"Oh, Brian," Gallowstree reasserted himself with verve, "you're hardly filling Tom with hope. Your numbers may be down, but I'm delighted to say that our attendance has soared in recent years."

"Yes, your attendance has soared. Because you preach fluffiness and cotton-wool and tell people what they want to hear!" Suddenly Brian was angry and each of his ninety-six months in Bruton was displayed as a separate wrinkle on his creased face. "You run your church like some kind of free self-help group. You're not a vicar – you're a guru!" The snarl was back, and now it was gnawing at every word.

"Well, you needn't be so aggressive, Brian. It's not very Christian of you, dear boy." Gallowstree tried to maintain a level of geniality.

Tom tried to shrink away from the conflict by fishing out bits of custard cream from the bottom of his mug.

As he left the church a few minutes later, the Dulux Colour Chart would have classed Tom's mood as "hint of excreta". He had been hoping to be filled with drive and vision for the area. Instead, he'd met two men of the cloth who had both thrown in the towel – and neither of them believed in what Tom was there to pioneer. One had become so disillusioned with the job that his only remaining hope was not that people would be saved, but that God would punish those who had blanked him. The other had become so admiring of his own sense of tolerance that the very concept of salvation seemed exclusivist and erroneous. Tom couldn't accept either view. There was hope for the people of this town, he was sure, and he was ready to give a reason for that hope. Brian and Gallowstree had misread the Good Book, but in a town where the library served up stripteases, was that really so much of a surprise?

"Looks like I'm on my own," Tom said aloud, his face tilting upwards.

He descended the steps towards the crappy little red Sedan. He groaned as he got to it. Where once there had been a driver's window, there was now no driver's window. It was simple physics, but he stared at it with confusion and disbelief.

Glass was smithereened all over the driver's seat, *Dux Ducis* had been taken, and so had the pack of Chewitts for the return journey. The Marvin Gaye CD had not been taken.

Frog's legs and dragon's teeth! Maybe Brian's right – maybe Bruton is a town singularly without hope.

He was using his sleeved-over hand to brush pieces of glass into a Morrisons bag (woefully under-equipped for the task of glass retention) when he saw Vicky, still perched upon the same bollard like an experimental piece of modern art. He remembered the prayer he'd promised to arrow up for her boy – a prayer which remained bequivered in his soul. Resolutely, Tom dropped the Morrisons bag and retook the stone steps three at a time. Brian and Revd Gallowstree were gesticulating wildly at one another in the lobby, in a style reminiscent of amateur *capoeira*. They stopped when Tom appeared.

"Brian, can I use your church? I've got work to do." Without waiting for a response, Tom hurried into the archaic hall with its nailed-down pews, and prayer books that looked as if they'd been unearthed at Nag Hammadi. Dawn the cleaner shot a proprietorial look in Tom's direction as he made his way to the altar.

"We're closed!"

"Well, you shouldn't be! You're a church. God doesn't stop work when you do, strangely enough."

Tom stood by the altar and threw a grappling hook up to heaven on behalf of Vicky and her son. He knew he could have prayed anywhere, but she had made a specific request, and a yes is a yes.

Then he left the church, throwing a wild arm of thanks in Dawn's direction, and returned to his violated car.

And he smiled.

On such a lovely hot day, who needs a car window, anyway?

* * *

Back at Hillingthwaite House, boxes were being unpacked and Amy was building a princess's castle with the empties.

"What do you think of my castle, Daddy?"

"Oh, it's so beautiful. If anything, it's nicer than our actual house."

Amy laughed. She was just old enough to understand her daddy's use of irony, even though, in this case, he wasn't using it.

"It's protected by a magic dragon."

"Oh, really? What's the dragon called?"

"Selina the cat."

"Selina the cat the magic dragon?"

"Yes."

"I see."

Rachel called down through the floorboards, "Tom? Tom?"

"Yes?"

"Tom?"

"YES!"

"Oh, there you are. We don't have any food. Can you pop down the road to the supermarket and get us some basic provisions? I've put a list on where the fridge would be if we had a fridge. Oh, and can you order us a fridge?"

"And some dragon food!" Amy called from behind her portcullis (two pairs of Tom's socks held in place by a book on sanctification).

"OK. See you later, girls."

"Oh, and Daddy?"

"Yes?"

"Selina has done a dragon wee behind the castle."

Tom skirted the cardboard stronghold and noted the small puddle soaking ominously into the carpet.

I might have to slay that dragon.

"Well," he said equably, "looks like your castle has a moat, too."

He added "detergent" to the shopping list, and left the princess to her magical, urea-tinged kingdom.

Tom made the short *spaziergang* to the local German supermarket, and started snaking down the aisles past the range of products available from all German supermarkets in the UK: bread, milk, hiking boots, fishing rods, etc.

He picked up the basic provisions on Rachel's list and joined the queue behind a woman who (as he would later find out) was his new next-door neighbour, a frail lady of eighty-two named Anne – the owner of the beautifully tended garden adjacent to his own. Their proximity on this occasion being mere coincidence, Tom was understandably ignorant of Anne's identity. Had he known that she was his new next-door neighbour, he would naturally have made polite, Gospel-prompting conversation. Equally, had Anne known that Tom was her new neighbour, she might not have looked quite so petrified when he followed her home.

The first hundred yards or so were fine, but once they entered the cul-de-sac of Dews Close and Anne saw that Tom was still eating up the ground between them, she furrowed her brow, quickened her pace and sprinted towards her house like the Usain Bolt of the octogenarian world. Tom had been absorbed in a daydream of Billy Graham's crusade to Bruton, in which he, Tom Hillingthwaite, was leading all those souls to salvation like a gold-medal apostle. Anne's Olympian dash towards her own domestic salvation snapped Tom out of his reverie, and he suddenly understood the predicament.

O.M.Gosh, she thinks I'm trying to mug her.

Before he had a chance to point out the mistake, Anne was ensconced within her house, the front door bolted and secure, the curtains twitching.

Oh no, that poor lady!

Tom had come to Bruton to love his neighbour, not to stalk her. He didn't want Anne quivering in her house at the thought of a perverse prowler; he couldn't allow her to think that he was a genuine threat to her safety.

So, naturally, he went to knock on her door.

He knocked and knocked but Anne didn't answer, despite Tom peering through the window, saying, "I know you're in there!"

Unfortunately for Tom, his relationship with Anne was to get worse before it got better. In fact the sole reason Anne had gone to the shops was to buy a Victoria sponge as a welcoming gift for her new neighbours – a gift she brought round later that evening.

Amy had been helping her mummy to unpack the mounds of clothes shipped down from Nottingham in the move, and so, as a treat, Rachel had taken her to meet some of the cul-de-sac's pets – including Boobies the dog and Catrina's albino rabbit, Mitsy – while Tom was trying on the new hiking boots he'd recently purchased from a local German supermarket. When the doorbell rang, Tom reasonably assumed it was his family returning for bedtime. Feeling quite dapper in his new footwear, he chose to play a chirpy fatherly prank on his six-year-old daughter.

Poor Anne. Before venturing out into the twilight, clutching the delicious cake, she had peeked through her curtains to check the road was clear of strange loitering men. When she rang her neighbour's bell, she certainly wasn't expecting the front door to open slowly, ominously, and then to have her pursuer leap from behind it screaming, "Heeeeere's Daddy!"

In a legal sense, Tom Hillingthwaite might not have qualified as a stalker, but he was top of the podium when it came to terrifying pensioners: a real world-beater.

Chapter 3

Avenger's Assembly

*I*t was Monday morning in Wessex, and this was the day when Tom's role as Community Builder on behalf of Jesus4All (formerly the Turn or Burn Gospel Coalition) began in earnest. After taking the car to the garage to have the window replaced, he had a school visit to make and a prayer walk to prayer walk.

The week had started with an anonymous call to their newly installed land line.

"Who can that be? We haven't told anyone our new number yet."

Tom lifted the receiver and said, "Hello?"

There was the definite sound of light breathing, but no reply.

"Hello?" Tom said again, but the line went dead.

"Who was it?" asked Rachel.

"No answer. Maybe a mime artist in distress."

"More likely it's Anne trying to take her revenge," Rachel quipped.

Rachel had been sympathetic about the stalking incident, and the previous evening, having soothed Anne with a cup of sugary tea and the offer of complimentary gardening in return for not going to the police, the two adult Hillingthwaites had sat down to watch *Batman Begins*. Tom's wife wasn't a fan of the DC Universe (or, in fact, of anything that had its own universe –"there's plenty of stories to tell in this one," she would say), but she was a fan of Tom, and so they had cuddled up in their damp house with the broken car and the cat wee on the carpet, and started to make a house a home.

Roundhouse Primary School, where Tom had his meeting that morning, was a "special measures" school, where it was sometimes joked that parents picking their kids up from Reception class only had to make the short trip from Year 6. Constructed during the 1970s, it was almost brutalist in style, and clearly prioritised function over aesthetics. It was also Amy's new school, and she seemed remarkably unfazed to be going into new surroundings. Whereas Tom felt like a middle-class fish-out-of-water, Amy plunged head first into her new social aquarium.

"Won't you miss your old friends?" Tom asked her on the walk from the garage.

"Yes, a bit, Daddy, but I'll make new friends."

"You take after your mother."

Tom had never felt that accomplished at making friends. When he left his previous job in the carpet retail industry after a decade's service, his work colleagues failed to mark the occasion with any sort of celebration, confining their well-wishing to a hastily bought card saying "Sorry for your loss", on which they had scribbled out the "y" in "your" to show how much they were going to miss him. It was the total lack of thought that counted.

He dropped his daughter at the gates and watched her skip up the drive towards the school, swinging her bag in time to whatever joyful tune she was humming (which was usually "Our God is a Great Big God" or something by One Direction). By the time Amy reached the main entrance, Tom could see her already chatting to some older children. Tom chose to hang around the school gates for a while and try to stump up conversation with the arriving parents, hoping he might reverse-inherit a slice of his daughter's confidence. Most of the other parents appeared too harried by life to talk, and seemed, Tom thought, to treat taking their kids to school like dropping off a parcel. The ones who weren't in too much of a hurry were a little wary of a man they didn't recognise standing at the school gates on his own, trying to spark up banter. After ten minutes of unsuccessful badinage, Tom strolled up the drive to meet the head teacher.

A tall lady, stylish and power-dressed, met him at the door with an efficient smile and matching handshake.

"Hello, Tom. I'm Kathy."

"Nice to meet you, headmaster!"

"Headmistress."

"Yes, I see that you're very obviously a woman, but I didn't want to patronise you in this politically correct age of ours. I know a lot of female actors, for instance, don't like to be called actresses."

"No, but they wouldn't be called male actors either."

Tom grasped his mistake and opened his mouth wordlessly. Kathy's efficient smile flicked upwards into a smirk, and a light switched on behind the curtain of her power-gaze.

"The politically correct term you're looking for is head teacher, although I'm quite content with headmistress. Tom, can you bear with me a moment? We've had a couple of parents come and warn us there's a guy at the gates acting suspiciously – I've got to go and confront him."

"Oh, no need – it was just me," Tom responded earnestly.

"It was you acting suspiciously?"

"Yes. No, I mean – I was just trying to chat."

Kathy's smirk vanished, and Tom could sense her trying to

remember whether they had received confirmation of his CRB clearance.

"Well, come in, and let me give you the tour."

Kathy led Tom through the traditional tour of Roundhouse Primary, which, like all similar institutions, smelled predictably of Dettol and bottoms.

"Does it bring back memories of when you were at primary school?" Kathy enquired.

Yes, all I need now is for Matthew Kershaw to hide my shoes at the bottom of the pond and then pull down my pants at the Christmas concert.

"I don't really think about it," Tom shrugged.

The only positive memory Tom had from primary school was those moments when, at the start of a lesson, the teacher would unexpectedly wheel in the TV and video. Sure enough, a slightly retro Toshiba decomposing outside one classroom brought a wry smile to Tom's lips.

Down one stretch of whiffy, tiled walkway, Tom noticed a decorative mahogany board with the heading "Roundhouse Top Achiever Prize". The list stopped after 2008.

"Did the gene pool stagnate around the mid-noughties?" Tom asked. Kathy's efficient smile reappeared.

"No, it was decided that making the children compete against one another wasn't conducive to a happy working environment. All our kids are high achievers, in their own way."

They're certainly all in the running for "Smelliest Bottom".

The last stop on the guided tour was the staff room. Through a pair of glassed swing doors they entered a wide area that had probably once smelled of cigarettes and chalk, but now smelled of cheap coffee and marker pen. Happily, it was the only room that didn't smell of posteriors, although the Dettol was endemic. A collection of teachers was strewn about, all looking miserable as they braced themselves for another calendar page of crowd control.

I wonder what the collective term is for teachers. A school, surely?

Kathy's entrance drew everyone's attention.

"Right, everyone, listen in, please. This is Tom. He's going to be—"

"Kathy, did you sort out the weirdo at the gates?"

"Yes, it was this man."

All eyes followed Kathy's pointing finger to Tom's face.

"This is Tom. He's going to be doing some Bible stories with the kids this year."

"Hi, everyone!" Tom said, trying to use the same sort of efficient smile he'd picked up from Kathy. It turned out to be inefficient, as its unveiling was met with grunts of disinterest.

A tall, well-defined man in Parachute Regiment shorts and an England rugby top (that was too tight to be comfortable, but tight enough to show the contours of his physique) paused between large gulps of black coffee.

"Great idea, Kath. I love learning about the Bible. Afterwards, maybe we could learn about the tooth fairy and Alfred the Great."

A couple of other men in sporting attire sneered and sniggered at this. *He's clearly their leader.*

"Alfred the Great was a real person," Tom said, efficient smile tied on.

"Look, mate," said the vacuum-packed meat in a rugby top, "I don't need you to tell me what's real, OK?"

"OK, but… OK."

The man in the Parachute Regiment shorts seemed to have taken an instant dislike to Tom. Constructed during the 1970s, he too was almost brutalist in style and, given his fine physique but terrible dress sense, clearly prioritised function over aesthetics.

"Oh, take no notice of him," said a woman who looked as if she'd forgotten to retire in 1988 and belonged in a nursery rhyme. "He's just grumpy because it's Monday. I welcome a bit of help diverting the kids – it's half an hour a week when I don't have to teach them."

Grunts of approval were heard around the room, and the staff returned to prepping for the day.

Kathy introduced Tom to some of the relevant teachers before the school bell rent the air in twain, and the staff all expletively trudged off to meet their weekly fate.

"See ya later, gorgeous," the army-shorts-wearing teacher said, winking, as his rugby-playing legs sidestepped Tom and Kathy.

Post-exodus, Kathy offered Tom a cup of very cheap, very strong-looking coffee (which his hatred of artificial stimulants led him to decline) and they sat and discussed Kathy's plan for utilising Tom's services. Aside from administering assemblies and leading the classes through Bible Explorer (a course Tom had been trained in as part of his evangelistic equipping), Kathy also envisaged using him as a one-to-one mentor for one of the more troublesome boys in the school. He would have the chance to meet the boy, Jake, after that morning's assembly.

After what Kathy described as "an organic envisioning session", she led Tom down to the Memorial Hall for the morning devotional.

The kids were herded in a class at a time. Amy trotted into the hall with two other girls, holding hands and already chorusing "Our God is a Great Big God". Tom caught her eye and she waved happily.

Tom's role that morning was to observe and to pick up some hints for his own assembly later that month. Kathy had told him that the remit for assemblies was simply to give the kids something inspiring to take into the day ahead. The six-foot pile of meat in the rugby shirt was the leader that morning, and he welcomed all the kids by telling them to shut up. Tom deemed that an overly hostile way to begin an assembly, but all the children instantly quietened down.

With his lack of learning, I wonder what inspiration he has to offer this morning – perhaps a mythical tale about the lost city of Milton Keynes? Tom chuckled at that, thinking it another good joke – the second since he'd arrived in Bruton. He made a mental note to share it with Rachel later that evening.

Tom asked the headmistress the name of the meatfeast.

"It's Pete."

Maybe he was trying to spell out PE teacher, and couldn't remember it all.

Tom grinned at his latest good joke, and decreed that "Petefeast" would be how he would henceforth think of the public-sector Adonis, although he had briefly entertained *le coq sportif*, concluding almost instantly that it would be taking things too far.

Petefeast's idea of a morning devotional was to play the kids a video compilation of semi-serious sporting injuries that he'd found on YouTube. Some of them were genuinely amusing, such as the one where a rugby player ran crotch-first into the post. Some – like the one where a cricket player had his teeth bowled out – were less fun. Perturbed by the graphic detail, Tom looked across at Kathy, who shrugged and looked coy but did nothing. Tom didn't want Amy being exposed to this sort of thing, and felt sure that most of the younglings must be terribly traumatised, not just by the injuries, but by the awful teaching methods. However, when the video finished, the whole school erupted into jubilant cheering and applause. Petefeast took centre stage again, and goaded the kids into continuing the applause for himself, pointing at his chest and then raising a single digit into the air as if to suggest that he was "number one". Tom hardly knew the guy, but he already came across as more of a number two.

"Remember, kids," Petefeast intoned, "you never know when you're going to have a career-threatening injury. So live every day like it's your last! Assembly dismissed!" At this, he lifted up his rugby top to reveal a tee shirt with "Live every day like it's your last" printed on it. The kids cheered again and then shuffled out, excitedly talking about which video maiming they preferred.

"Is that what counts as a good assembly these days?" Tom asked Kathy when they got back to the staff room.

"The kids seemed to like it."

"But that's because he showed them something their parents wouldn't let them watch! And besides, the message doesn't even make any sense. Live every day like it's your last? What does that even mean?"

Kathy smoothed down a crease in her corporette suit, and said, "Look, you'll be doing the next assembly, so it's a good opportunity to change the format." She smiled across at Tom, but the efficient smile looked more tightly strung than before. Another bell sounded and, in a Pavlovian response, the tautness left her face.

"Anyway, let's go and meet Jake, shall we? He's the lad you'll be doing some one-to-one with."

"Sounds great. Before we do that, though, can I show you Little Tom?"

Kathy looked briefly startled, and visibly relaxed with relief when she realised Tom was talking about the hand puppet he pulled from his bag.

"Sorry, Tom. I thought for a moment I'd made a terrible mistake being alone with you."

She shook with laughter, about 10 per cent of which was mirth and 90 per cent voided nerves.

"It's what my wife tells me all the time," Tom said, trying to brush off the awkwardness, and musing that maybe Little Tom might not be the best name for the puppet. (It was the third time that name had caused tension, and he'd only shown the puppet to four people. Rachel had just said, "Not right now, thanks.")

Kathy ushered Tom back down the corridor to Jake's classroom, her heeled boots clack-clacking authoritatively on the mottled floor. Tom was wearing soft pumps, which made almost no noise bar a limp slapping which failed to cover the sound when he emitted his own soft pump through nerves. As they approached the appropriate door, Tom explained to Kathy that, as part of his training with Jesus4All (formerly the Turn or Burn Gospel Coalition), he had been on a course about using hand-puppets with sensitive children.

"I learned that they sometimes help to draw the children out of themselves by making them feel the puppet is their friend," he told her.

"Yes. Just don't expect too much too soon with Jake. Puppets might not be his thing."

He repeated the fact that he'd been on a bespoke course, and Kathy smiled and raised her eyebrows.

"Look, Tom, I think you'll be great with Jake, but we've got to follow the correct procedures: nothing religious, nothing too autobiographical. I'm sure you're a man of many colours, but this is not about you. Here you've got to be 'the grey man'."

Tom nodded seriously.

As Kathy fetched Jake from his lesson, Tom loitered outside the classroom, waving through the glass at the form tutor, Mrs Quinn, who raised an eyebrow but nothing more. Tom had been warned that Mrs Quinn was a slightly officious busybody (by Mrs Quinn herself, strangely) and he wondered whether she saw his planned sessions with Jake as undermining her own authority.

The young lad who appeared was much smaller than Tom had expected. He had pictured the school troublemaker as having unreasonably well-developed muscles and a comic-book jawbone. Instead, the little boy was just that, and his clothes hung off him like a scarecrow's. None of his uniform was regulation, and it reminded Tom of the clothes you wear to pick up bricks from the bottom of the swimming pool. Without getting too close, Tom could tell that the clothes (and the boy lost somewhere inside them) reeked badly.

Even a scarecrow doesn't have to wear stuff like this. Maybe he could do with time in a swimming pool, Tom thought, and then rebuked himself for such flippancy.

"So, Jake, this is Tom. He's going to be chatting to you every week from now on. How does that sound?"

"Pleasure and a privilege to meet you, Jake," Tom said, offering his hand to the lad who looked bereft of pleasure or privilege.

Jake squinted up at him, then at his proffered hand, then looked back at the floor without saying anything. It wasn't that encouraging, but he still seemed infinitely happier to have Tom there than Petefeast had been.

"So, what sort of extra-curricular activities do you like, Jake?" Tom asked, with all the cultural awareness of a Puritan missionary holding up a Bible to ward off savages.

Jake looked totally blank. The lights were on, someone was at home, but they had no intention of opening the door.

"Tom means hobbies, I think, Jake – that's what extra-curricular means."

Jake shrugged and continued his tile-based vigil.

"I've got something you might like." Tom pulled the puppet out of its bag. "It's not very well made, and I can't remember where I got it. I've had it since I was your age. This is Lit– Barney."

"What's a litbarney?" Jake mumbled. Tom didn't know what a litbarney was, so, in a flourish of linguistic jazz, he amended the name to just Barney.

"I figured we could use him in some of our sessions. What do you say?"

No answer. Jake glanced at the muppet, then at the puppet he was holding, and nestled his chin back into his chest.

"Jake?"

"It's ugly."

"It's a 'he', not an 'it'," Tom corrected, slightly piqued. The course he had been on had never dealt with issues of doll gender discrimination. He already felt as though he was drowning in this new aquarium.

Kathy the headmistress pulled the plug, stepping in and ushering Jake back into his classroom. Tom looked forlornly down at Little Tom/Barney.

Whatever his name is, Jake's right – he is ugly.

On the bright side, Tom had at least followed the protocol: he hadn't got religious or personal. He never had the chance.

* * *

Back at home, Tom was recounting the assembly to his wife and daughter.

"Goodness knows what it actually assembled. A tower of vacuous nonsense, probably!"

"Very witty," Rachel said, without creasing her eyes in that way that people do when they genuinely find something witty.

"I mean, he showed them sports injuries! First thing on Monday morning! Is this the sort of school we've sent Amy to? Maybe that's just for starters. What's he got planned for his next assembly – a montage of public executions?"

"I wouldn't have thought that very likely, honeybunny."

"It was a funny video, Mummy," Amy piped up from behind a potato waffle. "It wasn't horrid like Daddy thinks."

"Don't talk with your mouth full, please, Amy," said Tom.

"And – get this – to finish, right, he encouraged the kids to live every day like it was their last!"

"Sounds like an inspiring phrase," Rachel mused. Amy (showing, in Tom's opinion, rampant favouritism) nodded along.

"What? Are you serious?"

The mutiny here is glaring.

* * *

Tom was woken at 7 a.m. the following morning, not by his reliably monosyllabic Michael Keaton alarm, but by the *dunna dunna dunna dunna* of his mobile ringtone. There had been another anonymous call to the land line in the middle of the night, and the disruption had caused Tom nightmares. The monophonic chirping of his Nokia wrested Tom from a dream where a young lad in scarecrow clothes had been holding a puppet, shouting pleas down an empty corridor. Tom was glad to be awake.

"Hello?" he rasped, with a mouth drier than a plague of sponges.

"Ah, Thomas, good morning! It's Harvey here. I expect you've been up for some time, ready for another day carrying out the Lord's work?"

Harvey was Tom's primary overseer at Jesus4All (formerly the Turn or Burn Gospel Coalition) and the most senior of the three head benefactors who ran the ministry. Someone more blasphemous than Tom might have referred to Harvey as the head of an unholy trinity.

Not wanting to exhume Rachel from her lie-in, Tom, who slept naked in tribute to pre-Fall-Garden-of-Eden days, stumbled out of bed and through to the landing.

"Hi, Harvey. I just woke up, as it happens."

"I see… well, we're not paying you to take a nap, Thomas." Harvey exhaled a strange sort of retching laugh, as though that particular function of his larynx had been dormant for some time.

"It wasn't a nap – it was my nightly sleep."

"Yes, yes, anyway, just wanting to touch base. How are you finding it in Bruton? Any fruit yet?"

"Well, no, not yet, but I've been scattering seeds. Already done some door-knocking, laid some good foundations, carried out a school visit." At no point did Tom mention anything about hunting down an octogenarian.

"Good show. Remember though, Thomas, it's bums on seats in the Kingdom we want to see! Ministry funds aren't what they were, so it's imperative that we capitalise. The harvest is plentiful, but the workers are few."

"Of course, Harvey. Yes, I'm excited about what we might be able to do here."

"Well, we're expecting great things from you, Thomas. More than that: the Lord is expecting great things. I'll be in touch again soon. Every good wish, then. Bye!"

"Bye."

Tom wasn't a huge fan of being telephoned at 7 o'clock in the morning, nor of being called Thomas, but, he conceded, the gents at Jesus4All (formerly the Turn or Burn Gospel Coalition) only wanted what he himself wanted: to save the world, one soul at a time.

Talk is fine, but it's what we do that defines us.

And he was on track. The social landscape in Bruton was even more rugged and barren than Tom had anticipated, but the first rule of sales, he knew, was to establish a need and then meet it with a benefit. In his role as Community Builder, he had already established a need: the Gospel. Now all he had to do was meet it with a benefit: also the Gospel. And he would.

But first of all, he would put on some pants.

Chapter 4

Far from the Mad In-crowd

It was Friday night, and while most normal people were traipsing home after a long week at work, keen to devour pizza and the latest HBO import, Tom Hillingthwaite was boarding a bus to go and tell a group of certainly unruly and potentially homicidal youngsters about what a friend they had in Jesus.

Tom had never really been "down with the kids", not even – in fact, decisively not – when he was a kid himself. During one phase in the early nineties, he had spent six intensive months shunning schoolboy interaction to train himself in the mystical art of yoyo, only to discover that everyone else had stopped playing with yoyos five months earlier and had moved on to having girlfriends. In fact, each teenage zeitgeist since his youth had dragged Tom along in its wake, and each time he caught up, a new craze, obsession or vernacular had already displaced it. (He had only recently mastered "Talk to the hand" as a means of "dissing" people, although he was yet to master the term "dissing".)

Nevertheless, this was important work, and the mission-based emails Tom had sent out before his arrival in Bruton had certainly paid dividends: numerous churches and organisations were getting in touch to offer him all the jobs they didn't want to do.

The name of this particular youth group was Burn – one of those bombastic names that churches across the West use to make their teenage outreach sound more edgy than it actually is. Other names include Impact, AngelFire, Deeper, Thrust, Refresh, The Power Hub and Not The Boys' Brigade.

Tom paid the £1.20 bus fare, adding an extra 7p as a tip, at which the driver sarcastically spat through the glass, "Wow, thanks."

"Let it be a blessing to you," Tom responded, impressively failing to pick up on the irony.

He chose a sensible seat half way back: he wasn't enough of a bad boy to sit right at the back, nor physically threadbare enough to sit right at the front, so it was an easy decision. The single-decker was empty except for a couple of likely looking young lads in urban-camouflage hoodies a few seats behind. "Likely", as in the sentence, "If you talk to them or look in their direction, they are likely to insert a knife into your flesh."

Their camouflage is flawed, though, given that I've spotted them… although they may be with others I haven't spotted. I'd better not say anything – there could be any number of them.

Tom sat quietly and surveyed some notes for that night's talk on his phone. It wasn't a top-of-the-range contraption (he'd downgraded his plan to reduce outgoings), but it did have a few apps: alarm clock, calculator, phone book, etc.

No doubt the two lads behind me have got jazzy, up-to-date i-BlackBerries, but I brought nothing into the world and I'll take nothing out – which is good, because I don't see this phone lasting the month, let alone through eternity.

When Tom looked up a few minutes later (he could tell it was a few minutes later because of the jazzy "clock" app on his phone) the two lads, like a couple of Whovian stone angels, had ventured closer without him noticing. One of them oozed into a seat behind him, while the other annexed Tom's own bench. There was an outside chance that they were merely huddling for warmth, but the heater on the bus was in mint condition, so that seemed unlikely.

"Show me," the youth next to Tom emitted in a voice four octaves lower than his actual voice.

"Pardon?" Tom responded.

"Show me the phone, man."

Tom may not have been totally *au fait* with youth culture (for one thing, he wouldn't have known that using the phrase *au fait* was out of bounds), but he wasn't so naive that he didn't comprehend the unambiguous situation here.

I am in the primary stages of a mugging, of which I am the victim.

"Giz yer phone, mate!" the young man wedged behind him growled. Tom decided not to suggest that, were he a real mate, he'd almost certainly let him keep the phone – or, at the very least, stick a "please" on the end.

Feeling his insides liquidising faster than a smoothie made with just bananas, Tom nevertheless tried to convey a dignified defence.

"I'm afraid I have no plans to show nor give you my phone, either today or at any point in the foreseeable future. Talk to the hand!" It was a resolute response, but his street-smart lingo didn't seem to deter them.

"Trus, man, we're tooled up. Giz yer phone." The pitch of the delinquent's voice was thrashing about all over the place, but the words were still menacing enough.

"I trust you implicitly," Tom insisted, "but I'm sorry, you can't have my phone. Let's all take a chilled pill, hey? You wouldn't even like the phone – it's hardly a top-of-the-range Tamagotchi."

At that moment, the hooded fellow perched next to Tom unzipped his jacket. This, Tom feared, was the bit where he had metal inserted into his flesh. He tried to remain stoical.

Most of the disciples were eventually beheaded… but that was for preaching the Gospel, not for having rubbish phones. I'm not dying for a Nokia.

Tom was about to blurt out that they could take the phone and that he didn't even get free minutes, when the jacket opened to reveal that the young lad was, in a very literal sense, "tooled up". Tucked into his inside pocket was a small screwdriver.

Inadvertently, through an instinctive release of tension, Tom laughed.

Ha! He'll have a job beheading me with that!

"Oi, joker, what's funny?" the lad shot back, trying to re-deepen his threatening voice. But the façade was broken and his mask had slipped irrevocably. As Tom's pent-up nervousness poured out in a continuing chuckle, the lad's face revealed what he was: a young teenager masquerading as a hoodlum.

"I'm sorry, cool cat," Tom soothed, trying to be sensitive to his assailant's crestfallen expression, unaware that "cool cat" had left the yoof-speak dictionary around the same time as *au fait*. "I'm not mocking you. Or dissing? Is that pertinent? Yes, I'm not dissing you… but a screwdriver just isn't scary."

"He's right, Henry," the second lad interceded. "The geezer's not made out of Meccano."

"Yes, and if I were, Henry, a screwdriver would offer the perfect threat. But as it stands, you're hardly going to be opening up a can of whoop-de-doo."

"A can of what?"

"I mean, with a screwdriver, the worst-case scenario would be for you to erect some shelving in a shoddy and half-hearted manner, and then for me to absent-mindedly walk under it, only for the whole shelf to collapse on top of me. Even then, we're talking, at worst, about a medium-sized bruise on the scalp."

The theft of his phone had been averted, but replaced, somewhat illogically, with a kind of mugging workshop – which Tom was facilitating.

"It's Hezza, man, not Henry."

Hezza's cheeks were definitely more flushed than those of your average low-life criminal.

"I do apologise, Hezza. Why did you want to take my phone anyway? It's not a very good one, and what if I called the police?"

"You couldn't though, like, if we had your phone."

"Yes, I suppose that's a good point. But you don't seem like a couple of BMX bandits. Why do you want to pilfer things at all? Is it kleptomania?"

"Nothing else to do, is there, Friday night? Too young to buy booze, brother's on the Xbox with his crew…"

"Don't you have yoyos?"

"What? No. So, like, y'know, nothing to do but rob."

Tom sensed a Red Sea of opportunity opening up.

"On the contrary, Henza!"

"Hezza!"

"Yes, of course. Look, fellows, I'm going to a place tonight where there's free pizza and drink."

"Booze, yeah?"

"No, mainly pop. But I've been led to believe there might well be some Shandy Bass knocking about, and I think there's a Playstation 360 as well, so all the bases are covered. You'd both be very welcome to come along."

"What games?" Hezza demanded, looking curious. "GTA.? Call of Duty?"

"Absolutely no idea. Why don't we all find out together?"

"Mate, are you a paedo?"

"Pardon? Goodness no! No, far from it. It's a youth group I'm talking about, run by the local church."

Hezza and his pal Jozee (or Joseph to his parents, who were both doctors) consented to come along to the youth club with Tom, won over by the promise of consoles. Tom, a half-life older than these quasi-streetfighters, was feeling uplifted. Despite the fear of doom he'd experienced on meeting them, he had stayed true to the call of duty on his life and had won them round. It was a far cry from his days in retail, but he was enjoying it.

As they arrived at Burn, Tom asked the two boys whether, in return for all the free food and gaming, they could pretend that they already knew him, and knew him to be "a good egg". Accordingly, when the three of them walked in, Tom appeared to be shielded by two rapping bodyguards. Jozee and Hezza, who were slightly older than the rest of the group, went ahead of Tom and started triumphally beatboxing and making the sound of gunfire as they announced him into the hall.

"Make way, make way for my man Tom, yo. He's a G round 'ere and he ain't no paedo. Hashtag Boom!"

The kids at Burn seemed to offer Tom a wary respect that night, and after pizza and Shandy Bass all round, he gave a short talk about how Jesus offers people a better way to live.

"The thief comes to steal and destroy," he announced, staring ominously at his two would-be muggers, "but Jesus came so that we might have fullness of life."

Jozee and Hezza seemed to be listening attentively, and Tom felt quite emotional when they said they'd definitely be back.

I can really sense GTA – God's Theological Anointing.

He got a call the next day from one of the other youth workers, to say that the cashbox had been prised open with a screwdriver and all the tuck shop money taken. Tom was initially distressed and hurt; he had been played like a Playstation 360, and it had all GTA – Gone Terribly Awry.

But after some thought, he decided that little acorns don't grow into strong oaks overnight – and only angels have haloes. Henry and Joseph just needed to hear more about Jesus… and to have any DIY implements removed upon entry.

* * *

When a new manager comes into a struggling business, his or her first job is not to make wholesale changes, but rather to consolidate what is good and use that as a firm footing from which to climb. "The stairway to heaven is carpeted," they used to say at No Rugrets, Tom's old company. He would often add the phrase "and by grace through faith" to that epithet, but people had usually gone back to work by then.

Tom didn't see himself as being in Bruton to cast aspersions on the outreach work that fellow saints were currently doing. He wanted to partner organically with the efforts already being made. And so, one evening, after a tea of chicken kiev and chips and salad and an extra chicken kiev, he headed over to Bruton Pentecostal Church for their monthly social outreach evening. He circuited Dews Close, hoping that a bit of neighbourly door-knocking might drum up a crowd. Sadly, the people behind every knocked door knocked him back, claiming busyness or, in Wayne the Tattooligan's case, a total lack of interest. The other neighbours were too British to admit disinclination, and so said things like "Sounds lovely, but I've already got plans" and "Make sure to let me know about the next one". They then withdrew to workshop a new set of excuses for next time. The truth, unknown to Tom, was that Anne still shuddered slightly at the sight of him, while

Not-Carl didn't want Tom talking to Catrina when he wasn't around.

Ironically, the Kung-Fu Gardener (who, Anne had told Rachel, who had told Tom, was called Blake), *would* actually have accepted the invitation. But then, he had spent a full two hours that day arguing with a settee, so the fact that Tom was too fearful to approach him was perhaps a blessing – in the very clever disguise of an evangelist too petrified to evangelise.

Bruton Pentecostal Church was a panelled wooden structure that was more of a fall-downing than a building. It had once been home to the Bruton Home Guard, and looked as if it should have been phased out along with rationing. In the single-glazed window there was a poster which declared: "All welcome! Monthly Social. Fun and Games and Refreshments!! All welcome!!!"

There seemed to be a big emphasis on everyone being welcome, which Tom applauded, but with that in mind, he wondered why the solitary poster they did have was inside the building, facing inwards.

Maybe everyone is welcome, but they only really want people with heightened prophetic abilities. Tom chuckled at that. *I must remember to write some of these good jokes down and tell them at parties.*

He wondered whether his quip might be close to the truth when he entered a slightly stuffy hall and found, seated around a large circular banqueting table, a grand total of four pensioners – a couple of whom might well have been founding members of the Bruton Home Guard, or the island nation of Britannia. The scene was redolent of a modern-day reunion of King Arthur's court, although one never hears stories of "Merlin and the Beetle Drive", which was the storyline unfolding here. Hastily, Tom mentally assigned a knightly name to each one of the party, before the head of the group welcomed him and bade him take a seat at the round table.

"You can be the fifth beetle!" he exclaimed, and everyone who understood the joke laughed. Tom wouldn't be writing that one down.

The refreshments, which had merited two whole exclamation marks on the scant publicity, consisted of custard creams and weak tea or coffee. Tom drank neither tea nor coffee, and he hated custard creams — cruelly labelling them albino bourbons to teach them a lesson. Yet his theory about terrible biscuits and church growth seemed to be gaining evidential weight. Merlin, the leader (who did actually look like Merlin. Or Gandalf. Or Dumbledore — any generic wizard, in fact), announced that tonight's fun and game was indeed a Beetle Drive — which Tom didn't think sounded like much of a game or very good fun. As he judged it, the whole advertising slant needed a rethink. Tom jousted with the idea of going home, but they seemed like lovely people and it was important to build relationships, and so he did his best to conjure up a look of excitement. He also assigned himself the pseudonym "Excalibur".

By the time the eighth beetle had fully evolved, Tom was diligently method-acting his role as Excalibur, in that he wanted to throw himself into a lake.

You can have too much of a good thing. You can also have too much of a Beetle Drive, which is any of a Beetle Drive.

Tom was right, of course. In the world outside the slat-panelled hall, it hadn't been played since Lot's wife turned into a condiment.

"Will you be coming back next month, then?" Lancelot, the youngest and most strapping at seventy-seven, enquired.

"What game will we be playing then?"

"Beetle Drive," they all said in flat, implacable unison.

"Do you never play any other games?"

"We like Beetle Drive."

"I understand that. But I'm not sure it's going to attract people from the community. This isn't the sort of game that people on the street are playing."

"Do not conform yourself to the habits of this world," stated a very pious Guinevere.

"Yes, and you came in off the street," added Gawain (who was actually a lady, but Tom's knowledge of the female characters in King Arthur's court was limited to say the least).

Tom didn't want to be confrontational with these ancient knights who had welcomed him so nicely and were eye-witnesses to the Roman invasion. So he thanked them for their company, wished them "good knight", and walked home plotting. In carpet retail, you listen to what the customer wants, and then sell them something better. Tom needed to find a way to show, not tell, these church grandfathers where they were erring.

"It was supposed to be an outreach evening," he complained to Rachel once he'd woken her up. "But it's not reaching out, it's shutting themselves in."

"Sleepy times now," Rachel said profoundly.

Tom couldn't sleep. He privately vowed to put on his own outreach night – one that genuinely engaged with local residents and didn't advertise in such a way that the only way to find out about the event was to already be at the event. He also vowed to learn more about days of yore, so he wouldn't have to give women male names.

"This is how we've always done it" – the seven last words of dying churches. "Shall we have another game of Beetle Drive?" – the eight words of already deceased ones.

Chapter 5

Unachievable Goooaaallls

*L*iving in a new place is often a good opportunity to reinvent yourself. Having so far failed to see any harvest of spiritual fruit since their arrival, Tom resolved that, in order to pick low-hanging fruit, occasionally you've got to bend the branches. Subsequently, he had ripened a plan to "branch out", spread his net so to speak, and join a football team.

Tom had never been good at football – it had always been something of a *bête noire* for him. People often complain about how they were always the last to be picked for a team at school. Tom Hillingthwaite would have loved to be the last to be picked at school. He would have happily, if he'd had that kind of budget as a nine-year-old, offered lucrative bribes in order to be the last to be picked at school. As it was, he wasn't even offered the dubious title of "manager" or asked to cut up oranges; when the games lesson came around, his teacher Mr Sterland would simply tell him to stay in the classroom and get on with something else, like drawing on the desk. He could best be classified as a hideous footballing leper.

However, none of the chaps he was going to meet that night knew anything about his shadowy sporting past. This would be a rebirth.

Tom turned up at the Kris Akabusi Sports Centre and asked for Mr Akabusi. When informed that the catchphrase-coining sprinter was merely the patron and not the Duty Manager, Tom scouted out the man who looked most in charge. Even someone as footballingly unbaptised as Tom knew that this was most likely to be a middle-aged man wearing a puffer jacket and carrying a bag of balls. He spied such a gent, and approached him with what he hoped was the right level of laddishness.

"Hello, geezer, are you the gaffer, innit?"

"Yep. Can I help?"

Quite proud of his opening round of words, Tom kicked on like the man about town he had never been.

"Yes, I'm here for the football auditions."

"Auditions? It's not *The X Factor*, mate. We're running some trials tonight, but you won't be asked to sing."

It became obvious that at the end of the day, Tom hadn't given his research 110 per cent, and so he thanked the ball-laden man and followed his gesticulation to the AstroTurf.

A group of very fit-looking men were warming up on the pitch, running very fast on the spot, shadow-boxing, and generally looking intimidating for someone whose most-played position was "inside, alone".

Tom was not what you would call fit. A doctor would call him chronically unfit, to which Tom would quip that he was too busy exorcising to exercise. Gamely, he tried to blend in with the exercisers, star-jumping his way from one set of goalposts to the other. It seemed to pay dividends, and when he had finished one of the shadow-boxers passed him a football, presumably as some kind of reward. Tom thanked him and picked the ball up.

"'Ere y'are, then," the passer exclaimed.

"Pardon?"

"Pass it over 'ere, mate."

Tom regarded it as odd that he should be asked to return the very thing he'd just been offered as a gift, but he duly obliged, kicking it with gusto roughly in the appropriate direction, sending his plimsoll flying as he did so. Some of the other lads started to mosey over, and before he knew where he was, Tom was involved in his first ever kickabout. He couldn't help smiling and feeling manly as the ball pinged its way from one set of feet to another. This was the sporting rebirth he had coveted; he was both exercising and exorcising childhood demons. He would have loved to see the look on Mr Sterland's face, if only he hadn't died from pneumonia in 1993.

After a few minutes of this kicking, the man with the bag of balls entered the pitch, now carrying a set of small cones.

"Right, lads, I'm Bill. I'm the manager of the Lamb and Flag Cossacks. Thanks for coming along for tonight's trials. There's about twenty-five of you, and we need twenty for the roster, so you've got a good chance of making the squad. We're just going to do a bit of ball-work, and then we'll split you into teams and have some eight-a-side."

"This is awfully exciting, isn't it," Tom whispered to the fellow next to him.

"Let's 'ave it," he smirked.

"Certainly," Tom said, handing him the ball.

"Wot ya doing?"

"You asked to have it, didn't you?"

"It's just a phrase, mate. Means I'm ready."

"Oh, right. Indeed."

This bloke, who Tom imagined must be called Gazza or Bazza or something similar, seemed to be fluent in all the salient lingo, and so Tom tried to man-mark him during the ball-work, in the hope that they would be picked on the same team. It worked, and when Bill the Boss split them up into eights, the two men were paired together.

"Dazza, can you take these boys?"

Dazza. I knew it.

Dazza drew his little group into a huddle and got them prepped.

"Right, I'll go in nets to start with. Nicky D., you stay up front. Tom, you OK to go DM?"

Tom tried to keep the sea of uncertainty from washing up on the shore of his face.

DM? What does that mean? Is he suggesting I study to become a doctor of metaphysics? Why would he need me to do that within the context of football auditions?

Not wanting to give away his ignorance, Tom simply said "Suretainly", and hoped he'd decipher it as they went along.

The teams lined up for the opening fixture, and the etiquette seemed to entail saying something mildly rousing to encourage one's team mates.

"Come on, then, let me have it!" Tom growled.

"Let's 'ave it," Dazza corrected him from the goal mouth.

The first match kicked off and Tom's team (whom he had secretly named Score-inthians) quickly went three goals down. Dazza kept shouting to Tom that he was out of position, but given that he wasn't in any way sure what that position was, he singularly failed to rectify the situation.

Worse, most of the other lads seemed to have come prepared with bespoke footwear for such a surface, whereas Tom was struggling with his plimsolls, which were getting slippier and more treacherous by the minute.

Score-inthians, belying their name, lost the first game 6–0, and Dazza gave them quite a colourful talking to before the next bout.

"Tom, you're trying 'ard, fella, but you're s'pose to be defensive midfielder. Stay just in front of the defence."

Defensive midfielder! That's what DM means!

If only Tom *had* been a doctor of metaphysics, he could have delivered expert punditry on the rush of filial gratitude that tackled him in that instant. Feeling more confident of where he was supposed to be standing, he performed a lot better in the second match, and Score-inthians earned a creditable 4–1 defeat. Dazza didn't seem that happy with another vanquishing, but Tom saw it as progress and told him so, only for Dazza to jeer something that showed he already had a DM: a Dirty Mouth.

Score-inthians and their specialist pump-wearing anchorman ended up playing, and losing, four matches. Tom did manage to find the net at one point, but it was with a loose plimsoll rather than the ball, and despite his passionate remonstrations Bill refused, somewhat unfairly Tom thought, to let it count as a goal.

At the end of the session, Bill the Boss gathered the squad together and said he was "chuffed" with what he'd seen. He declared that a list of successful candidates would be posted in the changing room for after they'd showered. Tom hadn't brought a towel with him, having failed to prophesy that he'd be expected to disrobe in front of the other men.

I'm a fan of hygiene as much as the next man, but my reward for a couple of hours' exercise will be a hot chocolate and a hotter Radox bath – not an encircling parade of dangling groins.

He gently informed Bill that he wouldn't be able to self-cleanse on site, and could Bill just let him know when the next training session was. Tom had been baptised of football, and now he just needed the subsequent confirmation.

Bill huffed. "To be honest, mate, you were by far the worst player here. You've got a good heart, but you're not really a footballer, are you? I mean, you honestly seemed to think you could score with a shoe."

Tom was suddenly punctured, like a cheap flyaway ball from a newsagent's bargain bin. He'd tried really hard, put in an honest shift "early doors" as Dazza might have said, and he felt he'd improved over the course of the evening, once he realised that D.M. wasn't a postgraduate course.

Bill saw his disappointment and softened. "Look, I'll keep you as a standby and let you know if we have any drop-outs, but for now it's a 'no', I'm afraid."

This wasn't the post-match press conference Tom had been predicting. Unsure of how to end the conversation, he invited Bill to the next Beetle Drive at Bruton Pentecostal Church, but Bill snorted and went off collecting bibs.

Feeling emotionally kicked about, Tom sought out his fatherly team leader to say farewell.

"O Captain, my Captain!" Tom warbled, quoting a nineteenth-century poem that Dazza couldn't have been less aware of.

"You wot, mate?"

"Thanks ever so for your pastoral guidance, Dazza. I'd follow you down a tunnel any day."

Dazza had no idea what Tom was talking about, but he wasn't a man who usually got thanked for things, so he gave Tom a brotherly punch on the arm, which really hurt.

Bill the Boss had said it wasn't *The X Factor*, and yet Tom left the Kris Akabusi Sports Centre feeling like a young hopeful who'd had his unfeasibly high expectations crushed. He retreated home to his man-cave, thinking of all the men in that shower, and how he wished he was one of them.

* * *

The following evening, the Hillingthwaite family was settled in its newly boxless living room. Everything from the move south had finally been unpacked, vases had reverted back to their original function as vases, and No. 3 Dews Close was starting to feel more like home and less like a gulag. It still had an oppressive spirit of damp, but the presence of their furniture and the removal of the cat urine from the carpet had given the house a gloriously non-Soviet feel. Tom had worked in the carpet retail industry for over a decade, and if there was one thing he knew, it was how to remove the smell of cat urine from a carpet. It was something of a party trick for him – one that, ironically, went down horrendously at parties.

Across the living room, Rachel was fashioning something intricate from beads while Amy was sprawled on the floor, working on a school project about maps, with Selina the cat perched regally on her shoulders, using Amy like a chair. Tom was relaxing in his luxurious leather lazy-boy chair, carefully reading his 1988 collector's edition Batman comic, *The Outsiders*. The Red Sea of lactic acid that had flooded his system after the footballing workout had refused to part at his command, drowning any hopes he might have had of walking for most of the day. He reflected that he would have been terribly ill-equipped for a job as a footballer. Or for a job as Moses. Initially crestfallen not to make the Lamb and Flag Cossacks team, Tom had since concluded that it wasn't the trouncing he'd considered it when he stopped to weep in a lay-by on the drive home. He had, on reflection, pioneered something new, made some new contacts, offered an invitation to a church event, and actually had a pretty jolly time. Even the resolute lactic acid felt like something of a badge of honour for Tom, whereas for most people it would have been a sign that they were woefully below the expected fitness level for a normal human being and needed to feel worried rather than smug. But in Tom's mind, he was equipping himself rather well in the job of Community Builder.

"Daddy?" Amy enquired in a confused tone, bringing Tom back to planet reality. She was looking puzzled at a map of the UK.

"Hello, down there."

"You know how we live here and Grandma lives in Scotchland?"

"It's Scotland, but yes, I am familiar with both those facts."

"Does that mean that when we go and visit her and Grandad Smelly, we have to go upwards?"

"Not really, no. And it's Smiley, not Smelly." Grandad Smiley was, as it happened, something of a cesspit, but Tom and Rachel both tried to play down this stigma in front of Amy.

"So it's not uphill all the way?"

"No, it doesn't work like that. North on a map isn't the same as upwards."

"And why does it always take so long to get there? It's not very far on here." Amy rubbed her finger up and down the map between Scotland and Wessex to show how easy it was.

"Yes, my love, but we don't travel by massive finger, do we?" Tom corrected her. "And that map isn't the right size – it's just a picture."

"Oh. Is there a map that's the right size?"

"Well, yes. You're on it."

Amy looked fascinated by the thought that she was standing on a huge life-size map, and returned to tracing her finger around the actual map, making the journey from Norwich to Penzance in a record time of 0.3 seconds.

As Tom returned to the comic and his daydreams of how well he'd integrated himself with a football crowd, inspiration pierced him like a needle of adrenaline to the heart (something he would literally need if he didn't start doing more regular exercise).

"I'm going down the pub!" he said to Rachel.

"Oh, no! Has the lactic acid gone to your head?"

Tom had never been in a pub in his adult life – not even when they were on honeymoon and he desperately needed the toilet and it was a choice between using the pub toilets or draining into a large Tupperware tub while Rachel shielded him with a beach towel.

"You're not having a breakdown, are you?"

"By no means, my love! I've proven myself as one of the lads, and now I'm going to go and mingle. You know, go into the rough places – like Jesus did."

"Right." Tom could see Rachel trying to find words that would both encourage and warn him without offending his pride. She had needed to do a lot of that over the course of their marriage – not least during the incident with the soiled Tupperware and the not-quite-large-enough beach towel – and he could spot it a mile off.

"The thing with Jesus, though, Tom, is that he was… you know… pretty good in social situations. Whereas you, my lovely husband, are…"

"…not very good in social situations?"

"Well, you said it – not me. I was just going to say handsome."

Frog's legs and dragon's teeth! She always does this.

Tom was immovable, both morally and physically.

"I hear what you're saying, but I respectfully say leave me alone. This is about Tom Hillingthwaite – me, your husband, Tom Hillingthwaite – making disciples and disciplettes. I've had very good reasons for never entering a pub, but the rules are different here. I can't just pick and choose who I share the Gospel with. Jesus didn't scour the libraries and coffee shops for his inner circle; there's no biblical evidence that Zebedee was sipping on a chai latte when the Lord came knocking. And besides, I'm one of the lads now."

"Which lads?"

"The lads. It's just a turn of phrase that the lads use."

"At least let me come with you."

"No thanks, my chosen. Jesus4All are paying me to chalk some souls up on the heavenly score sheet, and unlike football, this is not a team game."

Tom hauled himself out of his lazy-boy and limped outside like a wounded hero from a war where the major foe was muscle entropy. He carried a book, *Healing in the Spirit*, under his arm. Rachel had suggested that a newspaper might be a better way of proving himself "one of the lads" – whichever lads they turned out to be – but Tom ignored her.

"It's all about starting a conversation, Rachel," he assured his wife.

Tom had no idea that the last time a conversation about the Holy Spirit was started in a Bruton pub, the local news story ended with the words: "His family have been notified."

In his pockets, Tom also carried an oven-fresh batch of business cards that he had commissioned for occasions such as this. They were supposed to read, in a delicious bold font:

Tom Hillingthwaite: Community Builder/Evangelist.

Here to help grow new followers.

Call me for a chat on: 015 ** ******

However, the space allowance on the card was limited, and so the pubescent trainee printer, who didn't really know what a Community Builder/Evangelist was and wasn't being paid enough to care, had contracted the text into something he thought made sense. So the cards actually read:

Tom Hillingthwaite: Commun/ist

Here to help grow new followers.

Call me for a chat on: 015 ** ******

Tom didn't know this. Neither was he a communist. (He did go through a phase of wearing a beret at university, but that was because he liked French things, and not because he wanted to engender the downfall of capitalism.) The truth was that Tom was far from being political; he was neither staunchly red nor blue, so he used to describe himself as "purple" – a mixture of the two – until UKIP tried to colour co-ordinate with the floating voters. These days Tom referred to himself as "the voter of many colours".

Unsure which of the local pubs to choose for this momentous occasion, Tom saw Catrina's boyfriend Not-Carl in the garden doing some vigorous hoeing, so he approached him for advice.

Maybe I'll even convince him to tag along. A man who tills soil would really add to my street credibility.

"Hello… " (Tom realised with panic that he still didn't know Not-Carl's real name) "young sailor, milad. I be on the lookout for a local drinking house of ill-repute."

Tom didn't really want a brothel, even though that's essentially what he had asked for. Fortunately, Not-Carl was so thrown by the incongruous pirate voice that he didn't register. Tom chose to plough a different conversational furrow.

"I see you're doing some hoeing."

"Yep, well spotted."

"And through painful toil you will eat food from it all the days of your life, eh?"

"No, just putting in a rockery. Why are you talking like that?"

"I don't know."

The creases in Not-Carl's forehead indicated OMG.

"I was just wanting some advice on which pub to go to, to be honest," Tom managed to say in his normal voice.

"Oh, I see." Not-Carl stopped work and leaned on his hoe. "Well, there's the Waggon and Horses and Coach and Four."

"That seems quite a long name for a pub."

"That's two pubs."

"I see."

Tom dallied for a moment to admire Not-Carl's hoeing technique, in the hope that Not-Carl might offer to accompany him. That never happened, so he bade Not-Carl farewell with another dose of inappropriate seventeenth-century nautical language, and handed him the first of the new business cards. Not-Carl read the card and muttered something that was as inappropriate in the seventeenth century as it is now. Tom's jib clearly wasn't cut to Not-Carl's liking.

Alone, but now suitably schooled in the names of well-placed drinking taverns, Tom plumped for the Coach and Four because it was a marginally shorter trek, and because he was scared of horses. He guessed that there probably wouldn't be any actual horses in the Waggon and Horses, but he was virginal and wholly innocent in this business and wasn't prepared to take a chance.

He entered the pub and the man behind the bar nodded civilly at him. Tom tried to nod back, but used too much excited momentum and somehow toppled over into a bow.

Assuming that the waitress would come and take his order at some point, Tom took a seat at an available table, opened his book and started to read, holding the book oddly at head height in the hope of reeling in some questions about healing. Had he been holding the book in a normal fashion, he would have noticed that an old man with a broken nose and salt-and-pepper beard had appeared from behind a one-armed bandit and was staring at him from across the pub. Nobody seemed to pay the man any heed, and after a couple of minutes the elderly figure smiled at the book-engrossed Tom, turned away, and then ghosted out through the side entrance.

Twelve minutes after Tom's arrival, the same nodding barman who had greeted him so civilly called across, "You gonna order a drink, mate, or you just using our electricity as a reading light?"

"Eh? Oh, sorry, I thought it was table service."

"What? When was the last time you went into a pub and it was table service?!"

"Er… never," Tom confessed. He gathered his book, shuffled self-consciously to the bar and asked to see a menu. The barman's forehead creased into the outline of WTF.

From up close, Tom noticed that the man before him was arguably the hirsutest thing he had ever seen outside of nature documentaries. Every visible area of the fellow's flesh was matted with hair, to the point where it was difficult to know where the hair stopped and evolution began. His Gameofthronesian beard might well have looked "hipster" at one point in time, but was now somewhere in the region of "lunatic clansman"; it was so dense, Tom thought it could have been employed to smuggle Bibles into China. (It wasn't just Tom who found the rug-gedness overwhelming: the barman once ran naked through the streets of Bruton, but police mistook his nudity for a novelty Wookie onesie, and waved him on.)

The BarWookie took visual note of the book in Tom's hand and, from behind the huge beard, smiled: the same smile a crocodile uses when he spots a gazelle picnicking on the riverbank.

"I see you've noticed my book," Tom said, graunching his gears into outreach mode. "It's about the Holy Spirit."

"Oh yeah? Well the only spirits we care about here are the ones that cost £2.20 per shot, or £10 for a paddle on Funky Fridays. Order one or get out."

If this bloke is a Wookie, he's one of the more linguistically advanced, that's for sure.

It is factually impossible to segue from the phrase Funky Fridays into anything spiritual, so Tom judged that he just needed to order something. He only really wanted a medium-sized glass of finest H_2O, but there was a vein beneath the BarWookie's eye that was starting to fret and fidget, and he didn't want to kick off an embolism. Tom selected his next words carefully.

"I'll have a… pint of beer, please." He had meant to say half a pint, but he was nervous and still had half his brain trying to work on a bridge between Funky Fridays and some sort of Gospel hook.

"Certainly. What sort of beer?"

Good grief, this is taxing.

Tom had read somewhere that buying your first pint was seen as a rite of passage, but he had never expected to face so many riddles.

What's he going to make me do next – grapple a troll?

"What would you inbibe in my position?" Tom said ingratiatingly. The BarWookie shrugged. "I like a bit of Bishop's Finger."

"I beg your pardon?"

The barman nodded his foresty face at a big lever in front of him. Tom noted the label.

"Ah, yes, perfect – a lovely half-pint of Bishop's Finger."

"Thought you said a pint?"

"I did indeed – a full pint of Bishop's Finger, or if it's easier, two half-pints in separate glasses."

"That's not easier, no."

"Grand. Well, just… just the full pint then, please."

The BarWookie grappled with the lever, sluiced the pint and sloshed it on the bar in front of Tom, then looked at him expectantly. In the pregnant pause, Tom wondered whether it was comparable to when you ordered wine and had to taste it to make sure it wasn't off. (This is, of course, not what one has to do when ordering wine, but Tom wasn't to know – he had never ordered wine.) Furtively, Tom Hillingthwaite, "one of the lads", raised the glass to his lips and took his first ever sip of hops.

It tasted like a rotting log dipped in battery acid.

"Yep… yep, that's fine, thank you."

"I'm so delighted to hear that. Now, that'll be £2.75 please – or would you like me to hand you a bill at the end?"

"I'm happy either way," Tom replied.

"£2.75," the BarWookie stated, his voice thunking down like a hammer.

Oh, I see – that last bit was sarcastic.

In fairness, Tom had at least managed to refrain from calling him "sailor milad".

Now that he was at the bar and furnished with a tipple (albeit one that caused weeping and gnashing of teeth), Tom elected to mingle with the locals. By the window, three drunken maidens – their maidenheads long since drunk away – were giggling flirtatiously, while next to him at the bar was a gnarled pensioner who looked like granite. He wore a knotted and slightly frayed red-and-white scarf around his neck, which Tom guessed must be the colours of a football team. Sure enough, on the wall-mounted screen above his head a match was being streamed live into the pub. Tom set to laying down a conversational fleece.

"I hear their DM is pretty shambolic," he offered, pointing at the screen.

"What." There is no question mark there because it wasn't a request for clarification. A British man watching his team play is a singularly uncooperative creature – you might just as well ask soup to hold moral values as ask a football fan to chat after kick-off. Tom didn't know this, and persisted.

"Yeah, I've played a bit of football myself… had some trials… scored a goal… it was a plimsoll though, so it got revoked."

To use a football analogy of which he was currently ignorant, Tom's banter couldn't have hit a barn door. His conversational through-balls were being cut out by a defence of total apathy, and so he decided as a last resort to lump a linguistic long-ball into the box.

"Who do you support then, mate?"

The gnarled man turned his igneous face towards Tom and eyed him suspiciously, as though working out whether the Community Builder was looking for trouble and needed demolishing. He tilted his rubbly head almost accusingly as he answered: "Arsenal. Dyed in the wool."

Perhaps it was because he'd never heard that idiom before; or perhaps it was because the man looked befuddlingly archaeological; or perhaps it was the mere fact that Tom had chugged a thimble of beer that was now slaloming through the uncharted territory of his veins like rampaging pirates. But Tom was convinced the man had said he'd died in the war.

Rachel would tell him later that any normal person would have just asked the man to clarify what he'd said, and not, instead, look a bit frightened and enquire, "Which war, if you don't mind me asking?"

"If you don't mind me asking?!" Rachel exclaimed, choking with laughter, when he filled her in on the incident. "Of course, Tom, because that's a real trait of the undead – they're very belligerent about answering questions."

"I was drunk, woman!"

"So what happened then?" she asked, still trying not to suffocate on her own gusts of laughter.

"He shook his head and silently went back to watching the match of football, so I handed him a business card, then went to the toilet and extricated myself through the window."

"Like one of the lads?"

"Like one of the lads, precisely."

"Tom, I love you, but even for you that's a bit irregular." She wrapped him in a cuddle and used his shoulder to stifle a guffaw. Tom went to pour himself a full pint of the finest H_2O, and then headed upstairs to bed at 9.58 p.m.

Just like one of the lads.

During the night – at 1.03 a.m., to be precise – Tom's subconscious projected a dream where a young lad was standing outside a pub, scared to go in, waiting for something. It was a troublesome dream, which didn't fit with Tom's mood about his most recent adventure: once again, despite a less than salvific conclusion, he had taken heart from his boldness in entering the desert places. To keep the ball rolling, he was up early the next day to initiate his next evangelistic tactic.

* * *

They say charity begins at home. Tom would tell you that "they" are wrong and probably work in banking; charity, Tom would tell you, begins next door.

He was in the kitchen, having just answered the land line to another distressed mime artist – something which seemed as integral to the new home as the cloying damp. Filling a bucket with soapy water while Selina the cat looked on, terrified, his plan was to start a conversation about Jesus through simple acts of service. Rachel, gracefully eating a bowl of muesli, raised a finger (and accompanying spoon) of contention.

"Don't you think you should ask people before you start doing chores for them, honeybunny? They might be worried that you'll want something in exchange – like those people who wash your windows at traffic lights."

"I do want something in exchange, my chosen. I want them to know that God loves them. And you know what British people are like. You offer to do something for them and they'll just politely say 'no', even when they need it. We live in a culture that doesn't know how to receive blessings. Thanks for your input, but I think I'll just go my own way on this one. Although if you'd like to warm me up a chicken kiev, I wouldn't say 'no' – because I need it."

"Yes, because that wouldn't look odd, you munching on a chicken kiev like regular people do with cornflakes. Perfectly normal, honeybunny."

The sun was out, and Tom set to work. Taking a sponge approaching the size of Australia, he began by sloshing the soapy water all over Anne's Nissan. Entertaining himself by singing "I'm helping out" to the tune of "Shine, Jesus, Shine", he was having a lovely time, diminished only negligibly by the non-arrival of a warmed-through chicken kiev. Tom spent a good forty minutes on the washing, and then, as the rays of the sun steam-dried the car's paintwork, he chamois-leathered the flip out of it to the glory of God.

It's the little details that touch people's hearts.

As he finished adding a sheen to the last of the hubcaps, drenched from splashback, his hands and knees pocked from working at tarmac level, he crouched by the offside wheels and surveyed his handiwork. And he saw that it was good. Picturing the look of gratitude on Anne's face, he jumped to his feet in triumph, shouting, "Mission accomplished!" What his roadside vision hadn't allowed for was the sight of Anne, the octogenarian stalkee, leaving her house and tottering her way across the pavement towards the little Nissan, key in hand, on her way to the shops. As Tom leapt up, she screamed and fell against her hedge as if it was the rope round a boxing ring, then bounced back up as though keen for further punishment. The look of baffled terror on her face would stay with Tom for a long time hence.

Rachel, who had seen the whole thing while washing up muesli bowls, charged out of the house to comfort the pile-driven Anne. Tom tried to add a sheen of apology and let Anne know that when he had said "Mission accomplished", the mission was never to snuff out her life-force. But Rachel shooed him away with his own chamois leather, pinning him into submission with a flick of her eyes, and helped Anne back inside her house.

"Yes," Rachel would explain later, "it's the little details that touch people's hearts. But Tom, if the big detail is that you're jumping out on your neighbour on a bi-weekly basis, those hearts you're trying to touch might start needing emergency resuscitation."

Chapter 6

No Filter

*I*t was the day of his first assembly, and an opportunity for Tom Hillingthwaite to assert himself as an inspirational figure for the kids at Roundhouse Primary School to look up to – a beacon of light in their troubled childhood sky.

The previous assembly, delivered by Pete "Petefeast" Clark, had been surprisingly well received, but Tom was reminded that even Satan can masquerade as an angel of light. Consequently, his aim that morning was to show everyone present that there was more to pastoral guidance than sugar-coated rabble-rousing.

Tom had been obsessing about Petefeast's tee shirt with its vapid slogan, "Live every day like it's your last". Accordingly, he had prepared a talk on Lazarus, and how sometimes thinking it's your last day is counter-productive.

As he consumed a breakfast of eggs on toast (rather than just tepid bread) and opened the morning post addressed to T. Hollingsworth, he shared his aim with Rachel: to deliver a talk so incisive and motivating, the future barristers and doctors in the room would look back in twenty years and say, "Yes, that was the moment, above all other moments, when I knew what

I wanted to do with my life – and I've got Tom Hillingthwaite to thank." Rachel told him that he could do with lowering his sights, but Tom didn't like any analogy with a military slant to it, so he dismissed it out of hand, fishing into a boiled egg with one of his toasted soldiers (although, naturally, he called them "toasted pilgrims").

Tom had not slept well, owing to nerves and the residual pain from his football exploits, and so at breakfast he continued his trend of "firsts" by doing something he had never done before – something even more groundbreaking than marauding into a pub: he had a cup of coffee.

Tom had always hated artificial stimulants of any genre, and would often opine that, while religion was the opiate of the masses, coffee was the opiate of the middle classes. If, as with all the other drugs, the government suddenly made coffee illegal, Tom prognosticated a total implosion of the public sector, with nurses standing furtively on street corners as social workers shuffled up to them asking for three ounces of Colombian. A sort of black-market cafetièring.

However, the wafting smell of coffee had never been inhospitably received by Tom's nostrils, and, truth be told, he'd always thought the family cafetière looked really exciting. Besides, this was a big day and so merited a big exception. There was no inherent danger: he had managed to avoid alcohol for over thirty years, and the mere kiss of it against his lips in the Coach and Four had secured a three-decade extension to that agreement. So Tom had a cup of coffee.

And wow! It was delicious and warm and smoky and creamy, and he suddenly understood what people meant by the phrase "soul mate". And so he had another one.

"Sing, choirs of angels, this is good!"

"How did you measure out the coffee?" Rachel asked, taken aback.

"Using the coffee scoop."

Rachel put down her shopping list, opened the dishwasher and produced the coffee scoop, indicating to Tom that what he'd used to fill the cafetière was, in fact, an ice-cream scoop.

"Fear not," said he, for mighty dread had seized Rachel's face. "These are drastic times, and what do drastic times call for?"

"Prayer walks, you always say."

"Drastic measures!"

"Tom, be really careful. You don't even drink coffee and this is dark roasted – it's not a good idea to start with something so strong. Don't run before you can walk."

"Forget walking, Rachel – I feel like I can fly!"

Tom mounted a nearby wicker chair and leapt off. He hit the ground at the "yi-" part of "yippee". Then, totally unfazed by the instant refutation of his flying theory, he left the house, having first written "lots more coffee" on Rachel's shopping list.

Amy was a little later than usual getting to school that morning, because Tom had stopped at the local branch of Cheeky Coffee to get a cup of coffee. He loved coffee. In the assembly hall of Roundhouse Primary, he sipped on his coffee, reading over his notes as he waited for the kids to file in. When they did, Amy raced over to him and handed him a piece of paper which said, "God luck Daddy and Amys Daddy. Love Amy and Suki xxxxxxxxx." It was, Tom thought, one of the few times where a spelling mistake actually made something more inspiring. There was also a picture of a rabbit, which Tom found less inspiring, but it was better than he could have drawn so he was at least impressed. (All Tom's animal drawings looked uniformly as if they'd been dropped in toxic waste but had come out smiling.)

Amy took Suki's hand and they skipped off to sit down, positioning themselves centre-front – the best seats in the house – waving and smiling and sticking out their front teeth like rabbits. Tom gazed around and saw Jake enter the hall, tailing just behind the rest of his class, scuffing his feet on the floorboards. Rather than sit cross-legged on the floor, Mrs Quinn unstacked a chair and manacled him to her side by the doorway.

Kathy the headmistress power-entered with Petefeast, his quartered rugby top and maroon Parachute Regiment shorts sticking two fingers up to fashionistas everywhere. Petefeast shot Tom a look of feigned excitement (which Tom barely registered because he was thinking how much he liked coffee) while Kathy announced the new school day.

"Good morning, everyone!"

"Good morning, Mrs Bevan!" the whole school droned in unison – apart from one Reception lad, who mistakenly shouted out, "Good morning, Mummy," drawing insane giggling from those around him.

"Right, children, as you know, we have a very special guest with us this term." Kathy smiled over at Tom, who nodded with such gusto that it almost toppled into a bow.

"Now," Kathy went on, "part of what he's going to be doing over the coming months is leading some of our assemblies, so I'm delighted to introduce you all to Mr Tom Hillingthwaite."

The applause Tom was expecting, and which one usually receives in this sort of setting, didn't materialise. Undaunted, he put down his cup of coffee and looked out upon the mass of God's children.

Look at them, uncorrupted by the cynicism of adulthood – open to hearing how much he loves them.

Tom felt suddenly overcome with the privilege of being there, sensing that his spoken epistle might set so many pairs of tiny feet on a Damascene path towards Truth. He took a deep breath, and was about to start his address, when a boy at the front unleashed an unpremeditated yet devilish parp from his bottom.

One hundred and twenty-seven seconds then passed before all the children and a few of the teachers were able to breathe normally again, but it offered Tom the chance to slurp a few more sips of coffee. When a suitable hush had descended, he began.

"Good morning, everyone!"

"Good morning, Mr… " There was then a horrendous caterwauling as a hundred children made completely independent and completely flawed attempts to get his name right. There was a "Hollingthay", a "Hillythwack", a "Willywait" (followed by more uncontrollable giggles) and a "Daddy", which came from both Amy and the boy who had called Kathy "Mummy" – thus securing him, in an instant, a decade of excoriating mockery from his peers.

"Oh, thank you, what a lovely welcome," Tom smiled. "Now, today, we're going to be…"

"Are you going to show a video?" asked a be-cardiganed lad on the second row wearing odd socks.

"No, no, no video today, I'm afraid. I've got something even bet–"

"Awwwwwwwwwwwwwwwwwwwwwwwwwwww," chorused the room, including some of the teachers.

"Show that video what Mr Clark showed," said the boy with the trumpeting rear.

"Yeeeeeaaaaaaaaaaaaahhhhhhhhhhhhhhhh," chorused the room, including most of the teachers.

"Live every day like it's your last!" shouted a poor, impressionable soul.

Tom decided he couldn't proceed with his talk until he had poached and de-tusked this rather unwelcome elephant in the room. It might not be good etiquette to challenge a teacher in front of the kids, but God and the coffee were both on his side.

"Right, about this phrase that you were force-fed by Petefe– by Mr Clark last time. What does it actually mean?" Tom was being rhetorical, but this was a school and so a forest of little arms zipped up excitedly. Tom pointed to one of the older kids.

"It means make the most of every day, sir." Tom could see Petefeast nodding approvingly on the periphery of his vision. "Let the little children come to me," the PE teacher whispered to one of the other teachers, with a faux-modest shrug.

"But it doesn't actually say that, does it? I concur with 'Make the most of every day', but that's not what Mr Pete is asking us to do. He's beseeching all of you to live every day as though it's your last… as though when midnight strikes, you perish. That isn't a salutary way to live – going around as though you've seen your last sunset."

Tom wasn't really sure what argument he was brewing, or why he thought it would percolate successfully. Unlike the Americano in his hand, his thoughts were unfiltered. All he knew was that he wanted another cup of coffee and felt invincible.

"Nobody's asking the pupils to live as though they're not going to wake up in the morning," Kathy interjected, rising nervously from her chair.

"Well, then, why does he have it on a tee shirt? What would it be like if I treated every day like it was my last? I wouldn't have planned anything for this assembly for a start – I would have been too busy tracking down my father to say goodbye. And then, when I woke up the next day, I'd start the whole process again."

The future doctors in the room, along with the future barristers, baristas and spongers, sat in silence. The atmosphere had flattened like a flat white, an awkward disquiet floating around like curdled milk.

"It's just a tee shirt, Mr Hillythwack," Petefeast bowled from the back, mock sobriety covering what was plainly a smirk of derision.

"Well, it's a silly tee shirt," Tom batted back. "A better tee shirt would be one that said 'Live every day like it's nice, but you can probably expect to live on for another thirty to forty years'."

"No, it wouldn't," said Petefeast and thought everyone else in the hall.

"That wouldn't fit on a tee shirt," Tom overheard Suki say to Amy.

"Oh yeah? I beg to differ!" Tom stripped off his jumper and slung it to the floor, revealing a tee shirt with, bizarrely, that exact slogan. He had bought it on impulse while waiting for his business cards to be printed, but he hadn't meant to reveal it at all; it was intended more as a Luther-King-inspired silent protest for him to enjoy privately.

But Tom was committed now, and so he started chanting it, slowly, reedily at first, but growing in gusto and resonance as each micro-unit of caffeine osmosed into his spirit: "Live every day like it's nice, but you can probably expect to live on for another thirty to forty years… everyone, come on, join in… Live every day like it's nice, but you can probably expect to live on for another thirty to forty years – yeah!"

A few of the kids joined in meekly, but there was also some booing and suggestions from the teachers that what he'd written didn't scan very well as a chant. What had started out as a peaceful Tiananmen-Square-style protest had degenerated into the sort of carnage one associates with coups d'état.

"Right," chimed Kathy, slicing through the chaos with a domineering power-walk to the front of the hall, "can we all thank Mr Hillingthwaite in the usual way for leading us this morning?"

The kids dutifully applauded: the same sort of applause that accompanied public hangings in the 1800s.

This had been a disaster, a horror show. Tom had said nothing about Jesus, nothing about Lazarus, and for all his gripes about Petefeast showing the kids injuries, at least he hadn't subjected them to an actual death, which is what this felt like – and not a temporary Lazarus-style death, either.

The bemused and amused children were shepherded back to their classrooms, their facial expressions as perplexed as those of Lazarus's family when he checked out of the tomb.

Petefeast Clark, the former paratrooper, snapped to attention at the back of the hall, robotically brought his hand up in salute, then swivelled and marched off, spitting with victorious laughter.

"Kathy, I'm so sorry – that wasn't what I had planned," Tom confessed.

"Well, that's some comfort, at least."

Kathy saw how hopeless Tom looked, and softened her power-jaw.

"Look, I'm sure the children enjoyed it, and it was certainly eventful."

Like a shark attack is eventful, she thought privately.

"Don't worry too much. Come and get a cup of coffee."

"No, thank you – I think I've had enough."

Tom felt more wired than a complicated bomb in a 1990s action film, and didn't want to shred his nerves any further before his scheduled meeting with Jake. That decision was soon taken out of his jittery hands, though, as Jake's form tutor, the officious Mrs Quinn, appeared from Petefeast's wake at the back of the hall.

Mrs Quinn was forty-nine, but dressed as if she was twenty-nine. Her private hope was that the difference would be split and she would perhaps look thirty-nine. But she didn't. The body didn't match the fashion, and she looked instead as if she'd recently downed a vial of Polyjuice potion and hadn't had time to swap outfits. She slytherinned across the hall, one eyebrow arching upwards like a primed cobra, her bleached ringlets emerging from dark roots, to announce that Jake was too embarrassed by Mr Hillingthwaite's religious antics, and didn't want to see him today.

"Religious antics? Are those Jake's words or yours, Mrs Quinn?" Kathy power-enquired.

"I'm paraphrasing, of course, Kathy, but it's still the case that Jake would rather stay in class today." She turned her eyes and predatory eyebrow fully towards the headmistress. "Oh, and what a good choice of guest speaker you made – a masterstroke from our great leader."

Venom administered, she relaxed her serpentine eyebrow and glissaded back towards her classroom.

Kathy puffed out her cheeks, and Tom noticed that they had turned a shade of crimson.

"Sorry, Kathy, if I've made things awkward for you," Tom said, his own face colouring.

Kathy's eyes were fixed on the snake-like teacher retreating down the corridor.

"Mrs Quinn's been here for twenty-four years. She was the in-house choice for headmistress when the previous head left, and some people say the governors had promised her the job. But then I got it through external appointment, and she's never really made me feel welcome." Kathy's hands were busily smoothing invisible creases out of her skirt. "I don't know whether what she says about Jake is true, Tom, but I think it's probably best that we draw a line under today."

"OK… yes, OK," Tom agreed.

"Well, see yourself out, then."

Kathy gave Tom's shoulder the briefest of squeezes, then swivelled on her Gucci heels and returned to her office. Tom folded the piece of paper that Amy had handed him and stowed it in his pocket. If that was "God luck", he'd hate to witness the alternative.

As he left the building, there was a part of Tom that wished today was his last.

And it was all the fault of the coffee.

Chapter 7

The Uncaped Crusader

It was a few days after the dis-assembly, and Tom had decided that the complete failure of the event was down to the "powers and principalities" arrayed against him, and in no way attributable to the progressive unravelling of his caffeine-addled mind. The fact was, he was still a new creation in this job – a work in progress – and it wasn't reasonable to expect himself to traipse in and find everything soft underfoot straight away.

A plush shag pile carpet without the correct underlay wears out quickly.

Feeling patient in his tribulation, Tom was rejoicing in the real hope he had found in his new stomping ground. He was learning all the time and laying down spiritual lino, and though his plans for the junior witenagemot hadn't prospered, he had at least shown up and "stepped out". As they used to say in the carpet retail industry, "You can never count the profit on an order you never took." (Although they also used to wait for the customers to leave and then carry each other about on Persian rugs pretending to be Aladdin, so perhaps there were better sources of inspiration.)

Settling in Bruton had certainly opened a window onto a new vista of life for the Hillingthwaite family, quite at odds with the semi-rural Nottinghamshire idyll from which they had been uprooted. Tom was feeling confident that once the correct spiritual flooring had been laid, his steps would become surer and his failings less pronounced.

After all, falling onto a Persian rug hurts less than landing on a cold laminate floor… and the rug's more fun to ride.

Satisfied that he had applied enough contextual carpet analogy to his current locale, Tom boiled the kettle for his morning devotional.

Back in Sherwood Forest country, in their little village four kilometres south of Clifton, Tom would regularly sit in his front garden in the morning, reading the Word while watching squirrels playing kiss-chase in the overhanging trees and listening to the horses whinnying in the neighbouring paddock. On this particular morning in Bruton, by contrast, the beautiful scene at which Tom gazed through his window was that of a man beating up a bin.

As Tom's palate was diving head first into a delicious manna-like cup of Bolivian roast blend, he noted the Kung-Fu Gardener leaving his house in his traditional Chuck Norris regalia. Tom leant on the sink, intrigued.

It's a lovely day, after all. Maybe he's going for a walk or he's off to the shops… no, hang on, he's telling off the compost. Of course.

This was confusing. As far as Tom could see, it wasn't a malevolent bin. It hadn't been giving his own bins abuse from across the road, or flapping its lid lewdly at passers-by; it had, in essence, none of the traits of renegade refuse, and yet here was the Kung-Fu Gardener, out there bright and early to invade its personal space.

Tom had never witnessed a regime like it. To his relatively untrained eye, the Kung-Fu Gardener was employing the old jab, jab, swear-loudly-at-the-bin combo that Tom had not seen from any other top-level fighter. Nobody else in Dews

Close seemed to have been disturbed by this rather one-sided brawl, and the combatant himself seemed oblivious to Tom's observation. Instead, he began shouting, "Van Damme, Van Damme."

Tom had never seen a Jean-Claude Van Damme film (his knowledge of the "Muscles from Brussels" being about as loose as a United Colours of Benetton tee shirt from the decade in which the man starred), but he felt sure that not even a low-budget 1990s actioner would contain a scene of wheelie-bin violation.

It's hardly a hard target.

Concerned for the man's psychological well-being – and feeling mildly sorry for the bin, which had nowhere to run – Tom picked up the receiver of his vintage red bakelite phone and rang the police. He was briskly connected and the woman on the line said, "Is it Dews Close?"

"Er, yes."

"Oh, yes, this happens all the time – don't worry about it."

"But he's thrashing a harmless bin. He's turning recycling into a blood sport."

"Is he shouting 'David Carradine'?" Tom could hear her smiling.

"No, just 'Van Damme, Van Damme'."

"Well, you've nothing to worry about, then, sir. It's only when he screams 'Carradine' that there's a real problem. Thank you for keeping us informed."

And that was it. Sure enough, a few moments later the one-man Fight Club dispersed. The pummelling ceased with a final double impact, after which the Kung-Fu Gardener stopped shouting, saluted the bin, then looked defiantly about him and announced, in an unfeasibly gravelly voice, "Just taking out the trash." He went back inside, leaving Tom to his spiritual ablutions.

Tom straightened up from the sink, shook his head ruefully, and took a long draught of coffee.

That guy would go down really well at an assembly.

* * *

An hour later, as the wheelie bin was still licking its wounds, the entire Hillingthwaite triumvirate were seated around the breakfast table, about to tuck into *croque-monsieurs* – which Tom had taken a shine to during his beret-wearing university days.

"How do you like your eggs in the morning?" Rachel sang.

"I like mine with an easy yoke!" Tom chimed biblically, ruining the repartee with a bad singing voice and a worse gag.

"Can I give Selina my ham and have a *pain au chocolat* please?" Amy asked, curling her lip at the hot sandwich.

"No. She's a cat, not royalty," Tom spluttered through unexpectedly hot béchamel sauce. "And that *pain au chocolat* is Daddy's."

Abruptly, their family time was incised by the *dunna dunna dunna dunna* of Tom's antiquated Nokia. It was Harvey from Jesus4All (formerly the Turn or Burn Gospel Coalition) ringing up to inform Tom of a fresh, pioneering strategy that they wanted him to implement.

"I do hope I'm not interrupting anything?"

"We're just having a family breakfast together, Harvey, so…"

"Oh, sounds lovely. Anyway, how are things? How was the assembly?"

"The assembly? Yes, it was… er… there were a lot of good questions raised."

"Ah, splendid, splendid. And more generally? Any new sinners brought to repentance?"

"Well, no, not as such, but I'm still…"

"Come on, Thomas, you've been there a month! Our man in

Mercia only started last week, and he's already filling heavenly pews. Bums on seats in the Kingdom, remember – standing room only, young man."

"Well, Rachel, my wife, has had a friend come to faith."

"Ah, yes, but we're not employing her, are we? Anyway, listen, we want you to get out."

Tom squinted and put down his *croque-monsieur*.

"Am I being sacked?"

Harvey emitted a retching chortle that sounded like someone on the receiving end of an unexpected Heimlich manoeuvre.

"Sacked? No, don't be silly. Not yet. No, I'm talking about you doing some street evangelism, Thomas. You know, town square sort of thing, maybe a spot of door-to-door. Let's see you out on the street."

I wish he wouldn't call me Thomas.

Unconvinced by the logic of this *avant-garde* strategy, Tom, who didn't have a *bon appétit* for this mode of outreach, chose to challenge the order.

"I just wonder whether that sort of evangelism is a bit outdated, Harvey. And, dare I say it, intrusive?"

"Oh, so you'd rather leave people alone to their fate, would you? Let them go down with their ship, eh?"

"No, it's just that…"

"I understand that you want to be 'relevant' – that's a big thing for young men like yourself, it seems – but let's not get too cavalier about it. Do the simple things well and the harvest will follow." Harvey spoke authoritatively, each word robed simply in Cromwellian piety.

"OK, Harvey. Of course. I'll take Amy to school and head into town today."

"Splendid news! No pain, no gain. You're a salesman, Thomas. Go forth and sell the Word of God. And remember, the Word of God sells itself. Every good wish…"

Harvey rang off.

No pain, no gain.

Tom looked through the window at the rubbish bin, and no longer felt the same pang of sympathy as before.

At least you get to stay at home today.

Tom had known this order was going to filter down eventually – one of his training modules for the job had been "Street Preaching" – and it was the one he'd been dreading. He didn't want to do street evangelism. For one thing, the word "street" had been appropriated by the youth generation and now meant "cool" rather than "pavement". (In that regard Tom was not so much "street" as "country lane".) Beyond that, times had a-changed, as he waxed lyrical to Rachel.

"I agree that the Gospel is timeless, but the culture to which we present it is always shifting. For instance, there's a reason why we don't all go round dressed as roundheads and cavaliers…"

"Just go for an hour – have fun," soothed Rachel, trying to clear away Tom's now-cold *croque-monsieur*. She was as anxious as Tom about him going into public places and talking to people, but it was, after all, part of his job, and as his *aide-de-camp* she wanted to support him. "Do it because you've decided to do it – not because you're feeling forced."

It was the *mot juste* from his wife.

"Yes, you're right. And I am a salesman. I've just got to push the sale. Two for one on all salvations!" Tom erupted with delight at what he was sure was a very good joke. Rachel probably wasn't laughing because she didn't want to drop a plate.

Fair enough.

"Where's that *pain au chocolat*? I'll have it in the car on the way."

"Sorry, I ate it," Rachel confessed.

"What? No *pain au chocolat*?"

"Sorry – it's something of a *fait accompli* now, I'm afraid. I'll buy some more from the supermarket."

"And some ham for Selina, Mummy?"

The Hillingthwaite *ménage-à-trois* (in the purest, literal sense of the phrase) dispersed from breakfast to prepare for their respective days, Tom's stomach only partially full.

No pain au chocolat…no gain au chocolat, I suppose.

And so, that morning, Tom Hillingthwaite climbed into his battered old red Sedan and headed into the centre of Bruton with a sense of purpose and a packed lunch – including some scrambled eggs, which he had hastily cooked and wrapped in cling-film, so they now resembled a potential life-form. He also had a Tunnock's tea cake tucked into his breast pocket.

"Is that a Tunnock's tea cake tucked into your breast pocket?" Rachel had asked, remarkably accurately.

"No, no. It's simply a heart engorged with a love for the people of Bruton," Tom rejoined, with the cleverest comeback he would ever use in his entire life.

Bruton town centre was limp, leaden and lifeless, and had the feel of a quarantined penal colony or the sort of place student filmmakers use to shoot post-apocalyptic zombie flicks. Bruton had once been a thriving market town and the site of a regionally famous meat market, whereas these days The Meat Market was the name of the night club opposite the Methodist church – both of which were closed and boarded up. Tom reminded himself to be gracious and non-judgmental, and then turned a corner to see a man in double denim kick a dog.

I just hope the dog wasn't doing street evangelism.

The only shop showing any signs of life was Greggs, outside which a queue of zombified extras was swaying impatiently. Seeing no other signs of sentient life, Tom headed in the direction of the sweating meat, some of which was resting on metallic hot plates, some of which was queuing to get in. Since he hadn't had chance to polish off his breakfast, he planned to procure a sausage bap and marry it off to his scrambled egg. He stood in the queue, right hand in his jeans pocket, kneading the egg in its cellophane coating as though it was a cheap and unsanitary stress-aid.

A woman came out of the shop with bits of sausage roll trailing unseductively from her mouth. Tom guessed that she had had consumed a bit too much pastry-encased meat in her time, bless her orthopaedic socks. Down her left arm were a number of decorative tattoos, one of which said "Faith". This could be a positive conversation starter, Tom reckoned, although sadly a diet consisting mainly of Greggs and leftover Greggs had ensured that the woman's freely moving rolls of superfluous flesh were submerging, at intervals, both the "i" and the "h".

"Excuse me?" Tom accosted her.

"I 'aven't got any money for ya," she said from behind a sausage-roll barricade.

"I don't want any," Tom protested. "I'm doing some work for the local churches here today, and I saw your tattoo."

The woman glanced down at her arm. "It's a Chinese fertility symbol."

That wasn't the tattoo Tom was referring to. In any case, although his grasp of Mandarin was minimal, he nevertheless had an inkling that the characters on her arm were identical to those for chicken in a black bean sauce at The Golden Wok down the road.

"I meant the one that says 'Faith'," he corrected. "Do you have a faith?"

"Yeah, course. Don't know who her dad is, mind, but she's a good girl."

"I see."

"Yeah, I got five kids."

"Five?" *Maybe it is a Chinese fertility symbol.*

Tom didn't really give credence to that sort of eastern mysticism, though this was a theological stance and not linked to his entry-level sinophobia.

"Yeah, five. Kyle, Jeremy, Billie Jean, Faith and Megatron."

"And what about Jesus?"

"No, just Kyle, Jeremy, Billie Jean, Faith and Megatron – though it is hard to remember 'em all sometimes, I'll give ya that." She burst out laughing and a flurry of puff pastry cascaded from her mouth like cheap confetti.

I'm not really making any inroads here.

During the course on street preaching Tom had been instructed that, within this evangelistic arena, a good technique was often to use the sights and sounds of the surrounding area as hooks, and then latch them on to the message.

"Do you believe in God, Melissa?"

"My name's not Melissa, and I've not really thought about it."

Her name wasn't Melissa. She hadn't told Tom her name. For some reason, the name Melissa just sprang to mind and, thinking it to be a word of knowledge, he spoke it out. It wasn't a word of knowledge. It was the name Melissa.

Stop guessing people's names, Tom!

He ploughed on, his furrow less than straight. "Well, I believe in God, and I believe that he loves you. He loves you more than you love your Faith or... sorry, was one of the five a Michael Jackson song?"

"Billie Jean, yeah. Funny story, truth be told: I called her that 'cos before she came out I thought it was a boy. Then out she pops covered in guts – they had to do it through C-section in the end, right – and lo'n'behold, he's a girl..."

"I see, and... sorry, I don't understand the link to the song – does it contain reference to a troublesome birth?"

"Eh? Nah, silly – 'the kid is not my son'… yeah? 'Cos she's a girl."

This mission field was substantially boggier than a man who wore plimsolls would have liked.

Get back on message…

"What a lovely story. Anyway, er, God loves you. He loves you more than anything. In fact, God wants to come into your life and live in your heart… like that sausage lives inside its puff pastry."

That sentence was, empirically, the worst simile anyone in the whole of Wessex would use on that day, but Not-Melissa didn't react badly… or at all, in fact. Tom took that as a good sign.

"Meli… whatever your name is, God wants to write his name on your heart… like you've had 'Faith' inked onto your skin with a huge unsterilised needle."

The woman looked bemused.

"How much money are you after?" she asked. "I only work part-time, ya know."

Tom felt scandalised, and not just by her misassumption: she was chomping freely, and every time she opened her mouth he could see excited morsels of herbified intestine gallivanting on her bouncy castle of a tongue.

"I'm not after any money," he insisted. "What I'm offering is totally free. It's priceless. You'll never find it on sale in Greggs!"

"Ah, I wouldn't be interested then."

At this point, a voice from inside Greggs bellowed out, "Number thirty-three!"

"Ah, that's me pizza. Best go." And off Not-Melissa went, without a single allusion to the contextual Gospel presentation Tom had just unpacked.

Undeterred, Tom bought himself a lovely coffee and a bacon butty from the vendor (he'd gone off the idea of sausage for some reason) and scouted out a good spot from which to speak life to the culturally undead. There was a cenotaph at the hub of the desolate market square – a tribute to the brave men who laid down their lives that Greggs might open seven days a week – so he set up shop there. The actual shops that had previously set up there were now almost invariably derelict and inked in graffiti, that social tattoo – defiant statements of art in a society where art didn't sell unless it sold out.

In one corner of the square an archaic family-run cinema sat cowed and hunched, its doors barred from the outside by the demands of the digital age. In one of the more charming daubs, above the proclamation "Mad About Film", one graffiti artist had scrawled "Insufficiently".

Tom had designed his own graffiti. Certain street preachers, he thought, had a knack of putting the "demon" in "demonstrating the love of God" by brandishing big fluorescent signs, emblazoned with baleful messages such as "The wages of sin is death", or "Hell: hot enough for you?" It didn't seem to occur to some brothers in Christ that motifs such as these might not be the most friendly, and might even seem a bit off-putting to people on their way to buy Vienetta. Tom had decided, therefore, to go the other way and employ, not just reverse psychology, but also his talent for a good joke. So, following the phone call from Harvey – but after the Kung-Fu Gardener's matinee show – he had hastily mocked up a sign using a flimsy wall from Amy's cardboard castle. It was a sign that announced: "Don't listen to anything I say". It might not have been a Banksy, but Tom had never heard of Banksy and so the comparison would have been moot. He was, however, hoping that the use of intricate mind games would act as a hypnotic tractor beam for pedestrian curiosity. Sadly, as the next twenty minutes passed, Tom noticed that the flow of foot traffic appeared very happy to take his sign at face value –

the only effect of his mind games being that several shoppers mistook him for a mentalist.

In a change of tack, he flipped the sign over and wrote "Good at listening" on the reverse. The ensuing twenty minutes produced no positive contact whatever and so, definitively, Tom took the rewritten message and, with his marker pen, added "Insufficiently" as a prefix.

Nobody seemed interested. Most people saw him on the cenotaph steps and just walked on by, although Tom did notice numerous pedestrians going into shops that they hadn't planned to enter, while one woman turned down a side-alley to avoid him, then reappeared thirty seconds later when she realised it led to a dead-end and some rats.

By coincidence, Tom was hailed by the highly perfumed lady from No. 1 Dews Close, en route to treat herself to some Chanel. She wanted to know what he had done about the sewage issue, and who did she need to contact in the matter of road kill?

"I don't actually work for the council. I'm a Christian eva–"

"Yes, well, I can't stop – I think my ex-husband is having me followed." She tottered off on her heels, an impossible balancing act on expensive leather scaffolding, her musk leashed to her like an attack dog.

She's insufficiently good at listening, that woman.

The only soul who paid Tom any genuine heed was a lithe elderly gentleman with a broken nose and a salt-and-pepper beard. He appeared almost out of nowhere, and stood leaning on a lamp post, staring impassively at Tom. There was something uncanny about the fellow (Tom felt an intangible chill creep down his spine) but he neither approached nor heckled and, presently, he turned on his heel and disappeared behind Home Bargains.

After forty minutes of standing by the cenotaph, without a friendly Samaritan to offer succour, Tom was wetting his lips to sound his own Last Post when, against the odds, a reveille was called. From Tom's right, a man advanced on his cenotaph stronghold, intent graffitied on his face.

Tom suspected that the Spirit was finally at work, and swivelled to greet him.

"Do you have a question?" Tom asked, with a broad toadying smile.

"Yes, I do – could you move from my spot please?"

"Eh?"

"This is my spot. I come here every week. It's the best spot in town."

"I know – that's why I picked it."

"Yes, well, now you can just unpick it."

The candid complainant flourished a badge in front of Tom, which identified him as the head of the local Secular Humanist Society.

"Look," the disgruntled questioner continued, stepping up onto Tom's cenotaph, "I've no problem with you personally, but can you please move? I do this every week and I'm here today to talk about tolerance."

Tom hadn't wanted to tread on anyone's toes, but this man was being overly territorial. If he wanted an argument, he could have it.

If it gets nasty, I'll tread on his toes.

"Well," Tom replied, "you say you're here to talk about tolerance, but if that's the case… well, couldn't you be tolerant of me using this space?"

The man looked momentarily shell-shocked. "But what you're doing is intolerant of my right to be here," he shot back.

"Oh, so you believe in tolerance until you find something intolerant? So you're not tolerant of intolerance? That seems a little intolerant."

The man squinted at Tom.

Ha-ha, I'm winning.

"Well, what are you here to talk about?" the head of the Secular Humanists enquired.

"I'm talking about sacrificial love," Tom declared, with the smugness that accompanied a feeling of victory. The corner of his adversary's mouth flicked up into a smirk.

"Well, if you're so loving and sacrificial, couldn't you lovingly and sacrificially find another space?"

Tom hesitated at this clever salvo.

"With respect, if this is the best spot in town, I don't really want to yield to someone I believe to be misinformed."

"Oh, so you're only loving and sacrificial until someone disagrees with you? That doesn't seem very loving or sacrificial."

Frog's legs and dragon's teeth! He's using my own logic against me!

There was a long pause as, like two hikers reaching an impasse, the combatants tried to scrabble up the linguistic debris to find a breach. Presently, the man offered his hand.

"Martin Hartnett – it's tolerable to meet you," he said with a wry smile.

"Tom Hillingthwaite – your servant," Tom replied in kind.

The occurrence of anything approaching positive contact felt like a boon for both of them. Their respective smiles burst at the seams, and the two men met atop the intellectual battlement, laughing like loons.

"I tell you what, Tom, why don't I stand next to you, and we can make a friendly gladiatorial contest of it? You know – turn Bruton town centre into Hyde Park Corner."

Tom was quite taken with the idea.

"I see – like one of those gangster rap battles you see on TV if you've lost the remote and don't have time to change channel?"

"Yes! A rap battle… but for people with undergraduate-level philosophy."

"What a splendid idea, Martin! You're on."

So Martin Hartnett planted himself a few feet away, and they prepared for their duel.

As he unpacked his things, Martin informed Tom that he was really just trying to get people thinking about life, rather than waiting for it to peter out.

"The people of Bruton are generally lovely, but it's not the most aspirational place."

"No, I've noticed," Tom responded. "Just getting people out of their houses is a chore." A strobe image of Anne collapsing into her hedge flashed through Tom's mind.

"Agreed," said Martin. "I set up this Secular Humanist group after the Sceptics Society closed down. The problem was, they kept putting on free lunches, but nobody believed them."

It took Tom a few seconds to understand that Martin was joking, after which he apprehended two things: (1) few people had been genial with him since he moved to Bruton, and (2) he needed to remember that rather excellent joke and use it in future conversation.

And (3) I think I've made a friend.

Martin and Tom spent the next thirty minutes heckling passers-by with their respective world-views.

"I want you to know about a great truth today," Tom declared to an off-duty bus-driver.

"There's no such thing as absolute truth!" Martin cut across playfully.

"Which means that what he just said is, by definition, absolutely false," Tom hit back. The bus driver was flicking his head between the two of them as though watching a tennis rally that was both surprising and making him angry. Tom decided that the "absolute truth" smash he had just delivered made it 15–love to him.

"You drive a bus, sir," Martin served. "My friend Tom here thinks that only a few people can get on your bus. I believe we can all get on the bus and enjoy the ride together." Martin had clearly been on the secular version of the preaching course Tom went on.

He's using context. O.M.Giddy Aunt, he's good. 15–all.

"On the contrary, Martin, I think everyone is welcome on the bus – they just need a ticket."

30–15.

"And yet to most people, it seems that the ticket machine is old fashioned and rather difficult to find." The bus driver, totally indifferent to the mention of a profession that he actually hated (he had wanted to be a chef, but had no taste buds), turned his back and shuffled morosely into Clinton Cards.

Martin looked askance at Tom, and whispered, "Deuce."

The whole excruciating experience of standing in the public stocks, being pelted with rancid disinterest, was made infinitely more bearable for Tom by Martin's presence. They say there's safety in numbers – but they also say, "Live every day like it's your last." Tom would be quick to assert that whoever *they* were needed to be sacked and some new phrase-makers employed.

It would be fallacious to say that Tom felt safe while soapboxing. People were swearing at him, throwing half-eaten Greggs pasties... but he was only getting half the total swill he would otherwise have received, so that was a bonus.

Sadly for both Martin and Tom, there was to be no Game, Set and Match. Eventually, they conceded that play had been rained off by a monsoon of apathy.

"Although 'monsoon' would suggest a forcefulness of response, Tom."

"Yes, Martin. So more of a drizzle."

They collected their stuff, and then both Martin and Tom offered to buy the other lunch. As it turned out, there wasn't anywhere open that hadn't been investigated for poor hygiene standards and/or murder, and so the two friends sat on the cenotaph steps and shared a pork and apple turnover from Greggs.

Between bites, Martin cordially invited Tom to the next meeting of the Secular Humanist Society.

"We're not anti-God – we believe in loving people, and you seem to do that already. You'd be most welcome."

Tom thanked him and said he would be honoured, and then invited Martin to the opening of Rachel's new community café.

"There will be some God stuff, but the food will be better than this!"

Martin laughed, and promised he would try to come along.

Tom had ventured into town that day to serve, and left feeling he'd been emotionally sliced and backhanded. Still, in Martin, Tom had met an unlikely comrade – and that was the base-line.

He went home happy. ~~In~~sufficiently happy.

Chapter 8

Pain and Prejudice

It was an overcast morning, and Tom was back at Roundhouse Primary School for his second mentoring session with Jake. He had arrived early and, having smuggled two Tunnock's tea cakes out of the house, sat eating them in the car park with a cheeky coffee from Cheeky Coffee, feeling quite naughty. (The most rebellious Tom had been during his own school career was when a teacher had told him to tuck his shirt in and he nearly didn't but then he did.)

He wolfed down the marshmallow offerings and then, putting childish treats aside, he made his entrance.

Before he was able to head down the corridor to meet his young charge, Kathy the headmistress waylaid him and hustled him into her office. She was looking anxious, her fingers and thumbs rubbing together frictionally.

"Tom, please take a seat."

"Is everything OK, Kathy?"

"No. I really shouldn't be telling you… what's that around your mouth?"

"Well, it's usually my face."

Kathy used a teaspoon to show Tom his own reflection, and

passed him a tissue to wipe away the splashback from the tea cakes.

"Anyhow, Tom, I shouldn't really be sharing this, but when Mrs Quinn came to the Memorial Hall after the terrib– after your assembly, and told us that Jake didn't want to see you – well, I have since learned that it was all her doing."

Tom's mouth twisted uneasily.

"That seems a little two-faced."

"I know. Look, as I said to you at the time, I think Mrs Quinn has some bitterness about my headship, so please don't take it personally if she isn't that amenable. Just do your best with Jake and keep your head down." Her request fell somewhere between an order and a plea.

Kathy then sifted a file from a pile of papers on her mahogany desk and handed it to Tom.

"This is Jake's file. Again, you're not really allowed to see it, but if it helps you to understand him a bit better, then… well, to be frank, I'd love to see you break through with him. My own father was a lay preacher, so I do understand where you're coming from. Plus, I'd quite enjoy showing a certain teacher that I know how to run the school."

A girlish, mischievous grin broke out through her usually immaculate power-smile. Tom saw the girl behind the mask, and beamed back at her.

"Thanks, Kathy. You know, I'd love to help you find a local church that you could plug into…"

Kathy's face twitched unwittingly. "I'm not the good little girl that Dad wanted me to be, I'm afraid."

"None of us are good little girls, however much we might try to be," Tom replied earnestly. "It's about grace and forgiveness, Kathy, not good deeds."

But the efficient power-smile was back. The little grinning girl had refitted her mask. She gestured towards the file.

Jake's portfolio made heartbreaking reading. Until quite recently he had been a normal – if slightly unruly – ten-year-old, but the problems had started when his father, a man known to Bruton police, had upped and left over the previous summer. Jake had been almost unteachable ever since. From hurling books at Mrs Quinn, through fighting with other children, to an incident where he set alight *Harry Potter and the Half-Blood Prince*, Jake had deteriorated from a miniature gent into a rebel without either a cause or a clue.

As his eyes absorbed the information, Tom's heart dropped to the pit of his stomach, taking with it the colour from his cheeks.

Kathy looked at him, and just as he had seen the playful daughter of a preacherman behind her professional façade, she saw behind Tom's mask a glimpse of a frightened young boy.

"Are you OK, Tom?"

Tom sighed, looked around the room as though teleported there from somewhere else, and said, "Yeah… yes. I just really feel for him."

"I know. The parents of other children in Jake's class started putting pressure on the school to do something, so…" The telling look she gave him fell somewhere between hopeful and futile.

That *something*, as it transpired, was Tom Hillingthwaite.

"I'll do what I can, Kathy." Tom smiled a perplexed smile, lopsided with the weight of expectation placed upon it. He rose to his feet, shook her officially by the hand, and went to retrieve his secret weapon from the passenger seat of his car.

Tom had once again chauffeured Barney (né Little Tom) to Roundhouse, defiant in his belief that the hand-puppet would play an important role in Jake's rehabilitation. Tom was forbidden from exposing too much autobiographical detail with Jake, and so Barney could perhaps act as a symbol –

something not of flesh and blood that Tom could speak through parabolically.

I know Jake said Barney was ugly and stupid, but familiarity breeds friendship. Or is it contempt?

* * *

As Tom's plimsolled feet plap-plap-plapped their way down the corridor, his eyes took in the wall-mounted art installations outside each classroom. Junior Three had been learning about underwater life, each pupil painting a different fish – most of which were grinning – and writing an accompanying description. Infant One were doing space travel and, like every school class since the original moon landings, had been making primitive rockets out of toilet rolls and pop bottles. It was over forty years ago, but there clearly hadn't been a giant leap in the teaching of arts and crafts. It was charming, though, Tom thought, as his small steps plap-plapped him on towards Junior Two's classroom, where the presentation board displayed a photographic collage of Petefeast Clark teaching the pupils jiu-jitsu moves.

No art, no craft, just a gratuitous vanity project. Why does Kathy permit him to get away with stuff like this?

Jake, the *enfant terrible* of Junior Four, was already waiting for Tom in the slightly claustrophobic cubby hole allocated for their sessions, tracking the sound of the plap-plap-plapping as it got closer (and stopped altogether at one point when Tom, for no discernible reason, fell over).

"Hi, Jake," Tom greeted him, with a big fishy grin and a painful knee from where he'd fallen over.

Jake, who looked mousier and scrawnier even than before, managed a half-grunt.

I'll take that.

"OK, Jake, today I thought we'd do something quite fun. I've brought someone to meet you whom you might remember from last time…"

Subtly and slickly, Tom produced Barney from inside his jacket, then used his sleeve to wipe the Tunnock's chocolate from around the puppet's mouth.

"I thought you could just have a conversation with Barney, as though you're the only two people in the room. Pretend that I'm not here."

Tom had done a course on this.

"I'm not stupid," Jake mumbled without looking at Tom or Barney. "I know you're here – your hand's up its bum."

"Yes, but… well, just… er… yes, I see." On the course Tom had been on (at the John Calvin Centre for Ecumenical Mission) they had failed, through gross neglect, to devote any time to dialogue about hands up bottoms.

"Look, Jake, I know it seems a bit silly, but I'd love us to give this a go. How about if you treat me like I'm not here? You don't have to look at me or speak to me. Just talk to Barney. And if you don't like it, we don't have to use him again."

Jake's prolonged silence was like the glorious tolling of wedding bells to Tom's hopes.

"Finetastic. Here we go, then… "

Tom had been advised that the West Midlands accent was a good one to use for puppets, because it was the most non-threatening, and so Tom had been practising talking in Barney's dialect all morning – although it kept deteriorating into a sort of Jamaican patois. He was hoping that someone of Jake's age wouldn't notice the difference.

It was time for Barney to enter from stage right.

"Alroyte Jike – what gon warn… what's goin oorn… what's guin on?"

Before he could get the accent nailed down, Jake hammered

out with caged anger, "I'm not a little boy!"

"Orgh, I noo ya nat a little boi," retorted Barney, who was currently of Jamaican descent but living in the North-East. But Jake wasn't talking to him – he was talking to Tom. Suddenly Jake's anger was uncaged, and for the first time he looked Tom straight in the eye as he screamed, "I'm not a little boy! I'm not a stupid little boy!"

Snatching Little Tom from Big Tom's hand, Jake hurled the puppet into the cobwebbed window, shattering the artistic fourth wall and Barney's sponge pelvis. He stormed past Tom, out of the room, out along the corridor and down the school drive, his Salvation Army trainers scuff-scrape-scuffing all the way home.

Tom stood there immobilised. Mrs Quinn, witnessing the escape from behind the Perspex glass of her personality, came winding out of her classroom.

"What's going on? Why is Jake running away?"

"I don't know what gon warn… what's going on, I mean. I'm not very good at impressions, but… I think the lad's just hurting."

"I hope you weren't trying to make him religious?"

"Sorry? Make him relig– I was trying to help him open up." The extent of Tom's failure was dawning on him by the second.

"I don't understand how you could let him leave like that."

This was certainly true: Tom had been told about Mrs Quinn – and also by Mrs Quinn – that Mrs Quinn wasn't a very understanding person.

The teacher, her head tremulously rattling with a venomous mix of indignation and triumph, ordered him to go and notify Kathy.

Tom felt sick. What was he going to say to Kathy? The butterflies that flitted about his stomach as he left Mrs Quinn had been eaten and usurped by bats by the time he passed Petefeast's martial arts montage.

The plap-plap-plapping tracked along the corridors, across the Memorial Hall and up towards the staff room – an errant child reporting to the headmistress. Dispensing with formality, Tom turned the handle to Kathy's office and, without knocking, went straight in.

"Hello? Kathy? I'm sorry, but–"

There was a muted yelp and a grunt of panic.

"Tom, please go away!" A horror-struck voice came from the interior.

Tom couldn't see the headmistress. The blinds were drawn and her big mahogany desk was barring his vision.

"Are you hiding?"

Tom would normally have been first into the fray for a game of hide and seek, but this was no time for silly beggars.

"Tom, please, just let me…"

Too late. Tom peered over the rim of the desk and saw Kathy scrabbling around frantically on the floor. The man she was with looked at Tom with a mixture of hatred and apprehension as he adjusted his Parachute Regiment shorts and striped fluorescent rugby top.

"I… er…" Tom attempted to say.

"I… errr…" Kathy tried to help.

"Deal with it," mouthed Petefeast as he strutted out of the room, nonchalance not quite managing to win the firefight against fear for control of his facial features.

The following conversation about Jake then took place.

"Jake's gone home."

"OK."

"Bye."

"Bye."

As was now customary, Tom left Roundhouse Primary School feeling less than chipper. But this was different. For the first time, he suddenly felt he couldn't do this – this job or ministry, or whatever it was supposed to be. The unprodigal son wanted to pack up and go home – home to leafy Nottingham where the horses whinnied and carpets sold at £3.54 per square metre.

He was upset for Kathy. In fact, he was upset with Kathy; Petefeast was a married man, and an idiot.

Although now I know why that idiot gets away with so much.

But mainly he felt anguish at the situation with Jake. It was one thing to be shunned by adults, who have grown a skin of cynicism throughout their life. But to have a child react so vehemently to a bit of light-heartedness – albeit delivered in a horrendously inaccurate accent – slashed Tom with a pain that was deep and evocative. There just seemed to be no way through with the lad; nothing he had learned on any course was working.

I didn't mean to treat him like a little kid. But he's ten, he is a child – and to deny that will only lead to trouble. I know…

Tom's emotions were like a Tunnock's tea cake tossed in the road during rush hour.

Tom strapped Barney (bottom un-handed) into the car, and collapsed into his driver's seat like a marionette with its strings cut. He was about to start the engine, when something across the road caught his eye and tautened his frayed strings. Sitting on a bench, looking directly at him, was an elderly gentleman: the same elderly gentleman Tom had seen during his soapbox session at the cenotaph. He sat there, pawing at his salt-and-pepper beard, his gaze focused solely, unflinchingly, on Tom.

Nervously Tom got out, rested a hand on the top of the Sedan and, with an effort of will, returned the silent voyeurism.

Who is he, and what does he want?

The man's reappearance was unsettling, unnerving, but stopped short of being frightening. Despite the broken nose his face was kind, inquisitive – somehow other-worldly. Somewhere inside Tom a phrase was trying to come up for air, but never quite broke the surface.

Unsure of the etiquette for such an occasion, Tom nodded a curt greeting and climbed into his car. He rolled out of the car park, keeping the man in his rear-view until he turned back onto the main carriageway.

The old man never looked away once.

Chapter 9

The House on Haunted Hillingthwaite

The weather across the United Kingdom had started to deteriorate. The British climate, illegitimate love-child of an Indian summer and a Siberian winter, was whimsically volatile: one day the sun was out, the next day people were hoarding wood for arks.

The pathetic fallacy was not lost on Tom Hillingthwaite, whose own fortunes seemed very much subject to sudden changes in climate. Indeed, he was starting to think that any argument in defence of Bruton's salvific potential was itself pathetically fallacious.

Within the carpet retail industry, Tom had climbed steadily through the ranks – rising without trace, his colleagues would confide privately – owing to a strong work ethic and the reality that, whatever creed you hold, everybody at some point needs to buy a carpet. However, nobody in Wessex, so far at least, had wanted to buy what Tom was selling: eternal life.

You would have thought that was easier to flog than laminate flooring

He had left his carpet company, No Rugrets, in a strong financial position. Bruton Town was proving to be, rugrettably, somewhat spiritually insolvent.

* * *

"It was the way he looked at me that spooked me."

Tom had been unable to get the old man's second visitation out of his mind, and was reviewing its ethereality with Rachel while opening bills addressed to, among others, H. Tillingthwaite.

"Do you think he works for the police?"

"The police? Tom, you don't even cheat at Monopoly! When have you ever committed a crime?"

"I relieved myself into that Tupperware tub on our honeymoon, remember? I tell you, we were playing chicken with Lady Justice that day."

"Tom, honeybunny, pull yourself together. If you were in trouble with the police, the police would be following you – not some septuagenarian with a beard."

"Well, then, who is he?"

Rachel mused, her sleek fingers tapping out her thoughts morse-codely on the breakfast bar.

"Well, Hebrews talks about entertaining angels. And it's odd that this man has appeared when you've been feeling particularly low. I don't know, maybe God is just letting you know that he's got your back. He is good like that."

A spontaneous light illuminated Tom's eyes: the thought was warming. He had been in turmoil over Jake's exodus, and had woken in the night from an anxiety dream in which a young lad in assembly called the teacher "Daddy", then burst into tears.

The whole situation had been exacerbated by the fact that Kathy felt obliged to put Tom on a month's "gardening leave".

Kathy herself was also taking some time off through "illness", so Petefeast and Mrs Quinn had full dominion over the school. The number of voided tea cake wrappers on the garage floor was a physical manifestation of Tom's inner strife – his man-cave depicting a Tunnock's Gehenna. Consequently, the idea that God might be interceding thus, manifesting such a physical sign of comfort and providence, moved Tom to tears.

Could it really be an angel?

He thanked his chosen with a sloppy kiss. Then, with an ascension of newfound positivity, Tom veered his thoughts towards the day's agenda.

Unlike her husband, Rachel had been something of a social butterfly since their advent to Bruton, and had seen a number of her lunching ladyfriends either fly to faith or develop a strong fluttering desire to know more. Setting up a community café would be one way to help disciple her disciplettes, but Rachel had also inaugurated, with a minimum of fuss, a weekly prayer meeting chez Hillingthwaite.

Tom would be present for today's prayer meeting, and was hoping to impress the ladies with a winsome hosting job – as well as claiming an assist if any of them toppled over into faith.

As long as I'm there, it counts.

Tom was simply evolving his evangelistic strategy. Plan A hadn't worked, and neither had Plans B–F. But there were still twenty letters of the alphabet to go, and he could always switch to numbers after that.

He was at least bringing a guest of his own, having managed to pan some gold from his gritty town-centre outreach. During one chaplaincy-style trip around the place where the ~~magic~~ tragic happened, he had bumped into Not-Melissa, the Greggs-loving mother of five with the unfortunate Fa*t* tattoo. They had struck up a conversation in Next, and Not-Melissa (real name: Babs) had assigned Tom to oversee her boys Jeremy and Kyle while she contorted herself into a new dress. At some point, Tom must have mentioned that he was a medium, which, unbeknown to him, had convinced Babs to accept the lunchtime invitation. The perceived success of Tom's chaplaincy chatter had led to him dubbing himself, in that moment, the Archbishop of Banter-bury.

Tom had also sent word to Brian Child, the Baptist minister, hoping that the sight of fresh Christian blood might restart his ministerial heart. Tom had birthed his own brainchild: that he would add credit to his biscuits-in-dying-churches theory by accoutring Rachel's oversubscribed prayer meeting with an abundant array of luxurious soft-centred shortbreads.

Custard creams indeed! I'll show you, Brian.

Tom hadn't invited Philip Gallowstree, the liberal meringue-coiffed reverend, through fear that he might start praying to Darth Vader.

The turnout was slightly higher than expected, the women arriving in erratic single file, like animals at the Ark who hadn't realised it was a plus-one event.

If Jesus gets any more popular, this might need to be one-in, one-out.

Wishing to show off his manly assertiveness, Tom ferreted around the house to secure extra seating for all the bums on seats in the Kingdom. He returned with a revolving computer chair, a camping stool, a very small stepladder and a hefty box of unusable commun/ist business cards that were now being used as post-it notes and coasters.

(On discovering the costly and embarrassing print error for which her husband was culpable, Rachel had written on the back of one such card, "Try before you buy next time", and then posted-it onto Tom's forehead. "Ironically," Tom had responded, "a lazily printed business card is something that never would have happened under Stalin.")

Brian the Baptist turned up as promised, looking decayed

and wearied, the sins of the world contained in the bags under his eyes.

Babs also arrived, and came in carrying a cheese and onion pasty, a look of sombre expectation on her ample face.

"Ain't there no candles?" she enquired.

"No, the room's south-facing," replied Rachel breezily. "I think the natural light of day should be fine."

Rachel wheeled in a wonky 1970s hostess trolley, with hot drinks and a Babylonian tower of expensive biscuits. Tom unloaded the trolley, then offered it to Brian as a seat. Brian spent the next few minutes careering from side to side until he got his trolley legs.

Rachel had banned Tom from drinking caffeine, claiming that he'd become addicted and half-joking that his blood type, which had been "O", was now practically c-O-ffee.

Her initial plan of surreptitiously switching to decaffeinated had failed, when Tom uncovered the jar while truffling for tea cakes.

"A-ha! The Hillingthwaites have eyes, I'm afraid!" Tom had admonished.

"I had hoped that it would at least seem like you were drinking caffeine," Rachel had grimaced. Tom had punished her by spending a day putting dirty crockery straight back into the cupboards: "So it will at least seem like I've done the washing up."

Tom was now prohibited from drinking coffee altogether, and so while all the ladies were given draughts from the majestic family cafetière, Tom was handed a cup of milky fruit tea. The tea was the shade of a ginger man on the first day of a beach holiday, and Tom's heart sank accordingly.

The gathered throng chatted and nattered and, in one case, tried to stop his chair crashing into walls, before Tom climbed atop the midget stepladder and bullied off proceedings.

"Right, thanks for coming, everyone," he gushed, graciously taking the lead at his wife's event, "and especially Babs, who is new to all this." Tom raised a crumbling monster cookie in acknowledgement, while Babs shivered ominously.

"For those of you who don't know her," continued Tom, "she has five kids and six tattoos. Now, if we're all ready, in a moment of silence let's prepare our hearts…"

Tom lowered his head reverently and, when everyone else followed suit, he sneaked a long slurp of Guatemalan coffee from a neighbouring mug. There was dead silence, save for the intermittent scritching from Brian's wonky wheels. After a moment, however, Tom felt the shaky grip of Babs's clammy hand around his.

Bless her, she's probably nervous at the thought of praying openly for the first time.

Affectionately, the Archbishop of Banter-bury squeezed her hand. Taking this as a cue, Babs rent the stillness in twain, crying out in a tremulous voice, "Come to us, spirits! Come and talk to us! Are you there, Derek?"

Ah, now this is awkward.

With head still bowed, Tom half-opened one eye, to find all the other members of the group with heads bowed and eyes half-open. Babs's earlier question about the candles now made sense, as it appeared that she had confused the prayer group that this was with the séance that it absolutely wasn't.

"Are you there, Derek? Awake, spirits, awake!" Her voice had taken on a sing-songy eeriness, as if she were communing with another realm. She was the Kate Bush of the Dark Arts.

Fully aware that this was all his fault, but not wanting to erase Plan G from the drawing board just yet, Tom decided that the best thing to do here – next to hastily inventing time-travel, jumping back to 1977 and telling his parents not to open that second bottle of wine – was to try and segue into some genuine prayer. And so, when Babs next quivered and quavered with, "Come, spirits!", Tom followed up with, "Come, Holy Spirit!"

"We welcome you here, spirits!" Babs wobbled.

"You are welcome, Holy Spirit singular… It's one-in, one-out," riposted Tom.

"Yes, Lord!" seconded Rachel teasingly.

Tom continued his charismaniacal attempt to nudge Babs away from witchcraft with, "We're here, Lord," to which she added, "I'm here, Derek!" – immediately after which a loud snorting sound emanated from Tom's left. He panicked momentarily that Babs's chanting had broken a spiritual fourth wall and unleashed some kind of pig-demon into the room, but on opening his eyes he discovered that it was in fact his wife, laughing irrepressibly into her scarf.

It's all right for you – you've already led people to the Lord.

"That's quite enough, you fool!" Brian blustered, entering the fray and turning his fiery rage on Babs. (That was the first time a UK prayer meeting had ever been curtailed with the words "That's quite enough, you fool" – although it did once happen in Malta.)

Before Hades erupted completely, Tom stole another long slurp of coffee to moisten his parched mouth. Rachel was too busy laughing to reprimand him.

"What the hell is this, Tom?" Brian drove on, pivoting off his 1970s trolley, which tinkled out of the room like a bested chariot. Brian's ire inadvertently toppled the Babylonian tower of biscuits to the floor, which smashed and sent crumbs to the four corners of the room.

"Brian, please, there's no need for that!"

"Why have we stopped?" Babs asked, confused. "Was anything coming through?"

Just my P45 in the post.

"Barbara – that is your full name, I take it?" Brian was curt and terse. "I don't know what Tom has told you, but this isn't a séance. We're not trying to contact the dead – we're talking to God."

"God? I don't know if I believe in God!"

"You don't believe in God?"

"Not sure."

"But you believe in spirits?"

"Yeah, course."

Brian's world-weariness could have stretched round the earth twice. Tom remounted the miniature stepladder and tried to umpire the mediation.

"Babs, I'm sorry you feel misled, but I can assure you that God is very real, and we're here to talk to him today."

"Oh, OK." She seemed perfectly sanguine. "Can we ask him where Derek is?"

"Who's Derek?"

"My uncle. Died last year. He owes me money."

Another pig-demon was unleashed from Rachel's corner of the room, at which point Babs turned to Tom and complained, "But you said you was a medium."

"Eh? No… I… I was talking about clothes. We were in Next!"

"I know, but there's no way you're a medium – you're a large, or I'm a monkey's uncle."

"What relation is the monkey to Derek?" a miscellaneous voice asked, after which pig-demons were unleashed everywhere.

It was the only moment in Tom's life when he wished to escape to purgatory.

Although even that might not work here, as I'd be instantly summoned back by Babs and asked to hand Derek an invoice.

Tom's face had been left pig-demon red once again. Inviting

Babs had been his brainchild, and there was no way of crediting it to Brian.

Welcome to Tom Hillingthwaite: where the tragic happens.

* * *

Tom's time as a Community Builder on behalf of Jesus4All (formerly the Turn or Burn Gospel Coalition) had so far borne absolutely no fruit.

Unless it's that plastic fruit that I sometimes bite into by mistake in hotel lobbies.

He had known that the early weeks and months would involve a lot of seed sowing, but the field where he was scattering it appeared somewhat follicularly challenged. Not only were his seeds being eaten by crows or taken by the wind, he sensed that the farmer himself had been slaughtered by his own farmhands or hacked to pieces by an out-of-control combine harvester.

Despite constant attempts to engage people in conversation with a view to talking about Jesus, most of his conversations halted a long time before Jesus was ever raised. Subsequently, he never got round to talking about whether Jesus was ever raised. He was in a world he didn't understand.

And you always fear what you don't understand.

If he was totally honest with himself, which he wasn't, what made it worse was that the rest of his family seemed to have a natural anointing for evangelism. Amy, who was six, was taking her friend Suki along to Little Angels every Sunday at the local Newfrontiers church, while Rachel was the new, young, female, English, not-called-Billy-Graham Billy Graham.

It just seemed so easy for her. She didn't stalk her elderly neighbours, or walk in on people fornicating, or escape out of pub toilet windows.

I don't know whether I need a lighter burden or a stronger back.

123

Whereas Rachel had a natural gift for witnessing, Tom was forced to witness his repeated social car crashes from the driver's seat.

I wonder if there's an accident helpline I can ring for that?

Even Selina the cat had notched up one more salvation than Tom. Rachel had taken her to the vet – where she was rather oddly referred to as Selina Hillingthwaite – and the tabby had flirted with another cat, to whose owner Rachel had got chatting, with an invitation to her critically acclaimed, sell-out prayer meeting. The lady had come, enjoyed it, understood it wasn't a séance, and made a commitment. The cat, who had been raised Hindu, had also converted, or so Tom imagined in one of his sillier moments.

If it hadn't been for the angel sighting – the idea which Rachel had immaculately conceived and of which Tom was now convinced – then he would have been all at sea, his hook well and truly slung. But that single piece of divine affirmation had given his soul an anchor, and a sense that he should press on at full mast to fish for men and women.

Because he needed this to work. He had no trust funds, no pension. The modest savings he had accrued over the past decade had all been ploughed into this mission field – the same field where the dismembered farmer now lay mewing beneath the overturned combine harvester.

If this doesn't work out, I'll have to start lying under Amy's bed while she sleeps, whispering "Become a barrister" at regular intervals.

At this juncture, his training was nothing; his will was everything.

* * *

Rachel's new community café would soon be holding its official launch (with bonfire and entertainment), and so the Community Builder took to the pavement to do some invitational door-knocking. Nobody on Dews Close had yet become a Christian, so Tom had his heart, mind and primal urges set on beating Rachel there. He so desperately wanted to be Tom Hillingthwaite: Pillar of the Community.

As Tom crossed the threshold on another day's ministry, verbal invites in tow, the Kung-Fu Gardener was kicking fifty shades of grey out of his refuse.

"Nice day for a walk," the KFG called across between pummels, his voice more gravelly than a quarry basin.

"Yep," Tom replied, elaborately.

"Haven't seen any commies around, have ya?"

"Any…?"

"Commies. Y'know – communists. Enemies of the West."

"Oh… no… no, never seen… nope."

Tom made a mental note to incinerate the remaining boxes of botched business cards at the earliest opportunity. He also withheld the KFG's invite to the launch.

I don't want him mistaking the bonfire for compost and asking it to step outside.

Not-Carl and Catrina were at home but didn't answer, while the over-scented lady at No. 1 asked Tom what he planned to do about the road works on Williamson Street.

"I don't work for the council," Tom insisted.

"Well, who should I speak to, if not you?"

"I don't know – I don't work for the council."

She agreed to come to the launch, provided there weren't going to be any racists there, and what did Tom plan to do about them anyway?

Wayne the Tattooligan, responding to the invitation while berating his dog down the hallway, said in his traditionally non-jovial manner that he would be happy to send the whole family along – and might even be there himself if he wasn't too "****ing smashed on vodka".

"Finetastic," Tom responded, jovially.

He rang ahead before going round to Anne's house. The eighty-two-year-old had no problem seeing Tom; it was seeing him unexpectedly that had nearly shuffled her off her mortal coil. Having twice nearly sent her to a dinner date with St Peter, Tom was keen to cultivate, in Anne's mind, an image of him as a masculine Mother Teresa, and not a slightly effeminate Jack the Ripper. He took the opportunity while there, therefore, to ask Anne if he could carry out some literal cultivation, and trim her hedges before the summer fled completely.

"Oh… well, yes, I suppose you can. Yes, thank you. Will you give me time to get back in the house before you turn the hedge-clippers on, though?"

"Suretainly."

Anne led him to the utility room where she kept her stepladder. Tom decided to capitalise on the genial mood by once more unwrapping his gift for humour.

"You know, I have a stepladder at home…"

"Oh, do you not need to use mine then?"

"My real ladder left when I was a boy."

"Pardon?"

"Sorry, it was meant to be a good joke, but you asked a genuine question just before the punchline."

"Oh. So do you need the ladder or not?"

"Yes, please."

Tom trimmed the shrubbery that divided his garden from Anne's, waving from his hedgetop perch to Amy, who was up in her bedroom trying to teach Selina to count.

Tom hacked and buzzed and shaved and clipped, until he was happy with a job well done. Even if he did say so himself, which he did, you could have put a spirit level on top of that hedge and found it "bubblecentric". Anne, watching from the safety of her armchair, gave him an enthusiastic thumbs-up.

"You look like a Roman emperor at the Colosseum," Tom shouted to her through the closed window. "Anne Claudius, or something!"

"What?" Anne mouthed back.

"Never mind," Tom soothed.

"What?" Anne said again.

Rather proud of himself, Tom shifted the ladder to the opposite side of the garden. He reached the pinnacle, panting slightly through his exertions, and looked down to see Catrina sunbathing, making the most of the summer dregs. She also saw him, as did Not-Carl, who was sitting on a lounger next to her. The air around Tom felt suddenly sparse..

In Tom's mind, he was simply the sort of man who wanted to bless his neighbours with modest acts of service. To the two people lying prone in their underwear, he was the sort of man who spied on semi-naked ladies from other people's gardens, whilst breathing heavily.

"Would you be interested in coming to a community bonfire and café launch?" Tom enquired, his eyes helplessly drawn to away from Not-Carl's features.

The look Not-Carl gave him was the sort of ravenous look that Colosseum lions gave Christians – right before they ate them. Had Anne Claudius not already dozed off to *The Archers*, she would surely have been thumbing-down.

At least he didn't offer Catrina money as a blessing this time. *Maybe charity should begin, and end, at home.*

He went home to Rachel, feeling like Tom Hillingthwaite: Pillock of the Community.

Chapter 10

Doubting Thomas

*I*t was a clear black night, a clear white moon, and Tom was in the kitchen, trying to consume some meat.

It was a Saturday, the Hillingthwaite's traditional date-night, and Tom had hoped to relax with hoisin duck from the Golden Wok and watch *The Dark Knight* on Blu-ray (which is what Tom called standard DVDs).

He was feeling overawed and, in truth, spiritually oppressed by the pervading atmosphere of failure; every time he tried to build a bridge of community, some devilish sapper infiltrated his perimeter and demolished it.

He wanted three things. The first two were friendship and brotherhood; he needed allies, people he could talk to, laugh with, pray with. He had Martin, of course, but they had only met once, and Martin wasn't the praying type. Then there was Brian the Baptist, but since the Séance versus Religion extravaganza, Brian was blocking Tom's calls, while all the other local pastors were either too busy or too cool to hang out.

The third thing he wanted was to be alone: just him and his family, and nobody else. Tonight, he wanted to be left alone.

Instead, Rachel had snaffled them what no media outlet was calling "the hottest ticket in town": an invite to a "cocktail and nibbles" party – the result of one of her many flights of social fancy.

Rachel found Tom in the kitchen, lining his stomach.

"I need you to help me zip up this dre… Tom, put the ham away. There'll be plenty to eat at Angela's."

"Nonsense. I'm from Nottingham, Rachel."

"I know that. What's that got to do…"

"I've been to these dos before, and people go on about the nibbles and the canapés, and it's always a let-down. Do you know what people from Nottingham call nibbles and canapés? Not enough food, that's what."

"Look, I'm sure there'll be plenty – you don't have to regulate your intake in advance. Now step away from the ham and help me with this dress."

Catrina from next-door-but-one had agreed to babysit for the evening, but had insisted that Rachel notify her by phone when they were leaving the party, and also when they were entering the cul-de-sac, and also when they were about to come into the house. Amy was giddy about Catrina reading her *The Tiger Who Came to Tea*, and thought it was hilarious that Mummy and Daddy were going to a cocktail and nibbles party. As Tom grappled with Rachel's zip, Amy paraded into shot in her mummy's high heels, squealing with mock incredulity, "Cocktail and nipples?"

"Don't say that when Catrina's here, please," Tom ordered with a shudder.

"I'm squirmy that our daughter is old enough to make jokes about nipples," he confessed to Rachel through the zip between his teeth.

"Just be grateful that she's still too young to find a joke in the word 'cocktail'," Rachel replied.

Tom handed her the remains of the zipper from her dress, and she went upstairs to pick out a replacement.

Tom's own sartorial exploits had been no more auspicious. He had spent the afternoon in Bruton, drinking americanos and tracking down his costume in the charity shops that asphyxiated the town's hub. They were practically the only stores remaining in the once-charming market town, aside from a few big-name chains – their profits hermetically sealed by Slavic working conditions – and a handful of independent family-run outlets, which were bought freehold in the 1960s and hadn't closed because the owners were either too stubborn or too senile to recognise defeat.

And Greggs, of course.

He had passed a pleasant hour perusing the shops, collating his outfit (an approximation of Allan Quartermain from *The League of Extraordinary Gentlemen*). From the Mad Hatter's Hat Emporium (purchased freehold in 1963) he picked up a Stetson; from Oxfam, a pair of khaki slacks that only reached the bottom of his shin, but could be covered up by the knee-high boots he snapped up from Cowgirl. Had he been more observant while trying on footwear, he would have seen a broken nose and salt-and-pepper beard stroll past the window.

When he got home he laid his outfit on the bed for Rachel to see. She told him it was an odd ensemble and, more crucially, that it wasn't a fancy dress party. Once again, Tom had been incredibly efficient at doing the wrong thing, but he reflected, staring down at the thwarted outfit, that in none of the literary works involving Allan Quartermain does it describe him as looking like The Village People.

* * *

The Hillingthwaite Two arrived at the party. Angela, the hostess, and Rachel greeted each other like sisters – sisters who hadn't seen each other for years and had heard somewhere that the other was dead. Rachel introduced Tom as her husband, at which Angela fell into his arms, kissing him full on the lips. Angela seemed lovely, although she also seemed to have treated the party's alcohol in the same way that the tiger who came to tea treated all the packets and tins in the cupboard.

She's absolutely tickled pink on alcohol, Tom thought, using one of the few phrases in the English language that makes no noticeable sense as a synonym for drunkenness.

Angela offered to take their coats, struggling in her inebriated state with the concept that Tom wasn't actually wearing one. She insisted, however, and so rather awkwardly Tom removed his jumper and she pinkly tickled off to hang it up. Tom took the respite as an opportunity to tell Rachel a good joke.

"In terms of drinking, it looks like the hostess has had the mostest." He laughed heartily and Rachel didn't. Presently, Angela came staggering back with three drinks. She handed one to Rachel, but Tom declined, to which Angela responded by downing both remaining cocktails.

From the spacious sitting room down the hall, a sort of repetitive beat – which Tom assumed must be some kind of dance music – was seeping inexorably. Aside from Marvin Gaye, for whom he had always had a unique affection, Tom tended to dislike any song that didn't have the word "philharmonic" somewhere in the title; to him, dance music was the sound of society's hopes being punched metronomically in the face and groin, over and over and over again. Beyond that, Tom wasn't what one might call a talented mover: if Tom were the parent and dancing the child, Social Services would have long since been called in.

As the tenor of the pulse changed to a flatlining hum, Angela dragged Rachel cajolingly into the party, leaning on her like a mobile bar and shouting things like "Big fish, little fish, cardboard box".

Left on his own, and saved from having to go and mingle or pop his body, Tom ventured into the kitchen to make himself a coffee. Angela's husband, Archie, was already in there washing up party essentials, amid which was the most expensive cafetière that money could buy in Debenhams. Tom had never seen such a receptacle; it was tall and sleek and noble, and would not have looked out of place on an Abu Dhabi skyline. Archie set it down to dry on the worktop, a wafting shekinah of steam surrounding it.

After a cursory greeting and a tentative enquiry on Tom's part, Archie undertook to shoot Tom full of caffeine.

"Unleash your beast," Tom said, unaware of that phrase's full range of connotations. Archie received it with an irony that was never intended.

"Not drinking tonight, then?" he asked Tom.

"No. No, I've had some bad experiences with alcohol. The idea of getting absolutely tickled pink turns me off."

"Right."

"Don't supposed you've ever had a Bishop's Finger?"

"Eurgh, disgusting. Tastes like a tree with an electric current running through it."

"My thoughts precisely, Archie! So no, no beer for me. And besides, the alcohol's in the other room, and I can't stand dance music."

"I'm with you there, friend."

Friend? Really? Great!

"What music you into, then?" Archie asked mid-pan-scour.

"I like classi– er… Marvin Gaye."

"Marvin Gaye? Yeah, he is classy, I suppose. Nice one, buddy."

Buddy?

When the coffee had settled for a minute, Archie looked across at Tom with a conspiratorial glint in his eye, and said, "Fancy plunging?"

Tom had never been invited to plunge another man's cafetière before, and as he crossed the vinyl flooring (£3.49 per square metre) Tom realised he was sweating. Resolutely, firmly gripping the chrome handle and with a gently caressing authority, Tom forced the circle of gauze to the bottom of the glass cylinder. Archie smiled broadly. Tom smiled broadly back.

He dared to call me friend. I have another friend. Move over, Martin! … Sorry, Martin, that was uncalled for.

It was a deeply sensual moment – one which caused Tom to feel curiously dismissive of his long-standing wedding vows.

I think I might be in the offing of what I've heard is called a bro-mance.

"I love my wife very much," he added brusquely, for clarity.

Now that they were friends, Tom could, in all good faith, stay in the kitchen and avoid going to dance.

Archie is my rickety aid station in a jungle of Amazonian dancing women.

"So what do you do, then… Tim, is it?"

"Yes, Tim… hang on, no… Tom." Still reeling slightly from the profoundly spiritual moment with the cafetière, Tom was failing to vet with any real efficacy the words floating from his mouth.

"So what do you do?" Archie reprised.

Meaning to notify Archie that he was a professional Community Builder, Tom's tongue tripped itself up on the word "professional". Consequently he informed his new friend that he was in fact, much to his own surprise, a "professor".

"A professor? Really?"

Oh no.

Tom needed to think fast. This man had welcomed him into his home, and honoured him with the modern equivalent of a peace pipe. To contradict himself now would make Tom look facile or moronic. He knew himself to be both these things, but he could do without Archie, his new friend – *my best friend* – knowing that. So he said: "Yes, a professor."

"What are you a professor of?" It was a perfectly logical question, and so Archie looked rightly baffled when Tom scratched his chin and said, "Errrrrrrmm…" Archie was probably surmising – correctly, in fairness – that when you ask an actual professor what they've spent their entire academic life studying, they do tend to know. Tom's personalised petard had once again hoisted him off the deck of standard human interaction, but he was committed now. He took a long draught of the sweetly aromatic Peruvian blend, and looked out of the window for inspiration.

"Cats," he said, the lie catching in his throat.

"Cats? A professor of cats?"

"But of course."

"What specifically about cats have you researched?"

Tom could hear the sounds of raucous bopping from the adjoining room.

Anything not to join them.

"Whether they can dance."

"And can they?"

"No. No. No, it's been a waste of time, now that I think about it."

Through narrowed eyes, Archie looked at Tom in a way that no real professor has ever been regarded. In the same instant that Archie realised Tom wasn't a professor, Tom realised in a stringent, academic way that Archie wasn't his friend – and that his rickety jungle haven had closed.

Desperate to somehow redeem the situation, Tom asked

hastily, "Would you like to become a Christian?"

"No, thanks," said his former friend. It was a more polite declination than Tom deserved.

Reddening in the cheek, Professor Plumface thanked Archie for the coffee, and went to take his chances among the savage Amazonian revellers.

As he stood on the edge of the dance floor (which was just the lounge floor with all the settees pushed to the walls), tucking into an *amuse bouche* and feeling distinctly unamused, Tom at least felt vindicated in his prophetic words over the lack of proper food.

Any tiger coming to tea here would just head back to the zoo – or commit suicide.

Rachel was across the domestic discotheque, Macarena-ing with her friendship circle around a plate of salmon and cucumber skewers. She looked so pretty, so congruous… so normal.

Suddenly, through the mesh of dancing body parts, Tom perceived a sight that was both welcome and familiar. Across the room, standing on his own, was a vicar.

The man was dressed in Anglican vestments, obviously one of the "too busy, too cool" demographic that he hadn't yet met. Tom would need to traverse the gauntlet of the dance floor to reach his stranded comrade, and so he set off, trying to contort his limbs in time to the beat, dancing in a manner that could best be described as "Big fish, little fish, has anybody got a defibrillator?"

Tom reached his target and shook him firmly by the hand like a brother – a brother who hadn't seen him for a while but probably hadn't heard that he was dead. The other vicar was younger than Tom's thirty-seven years – perhaps late twenties – and he was tanned and in no need of a defibrillator.

"I believe we're in the same profession. Tom Hillingthwaite. Pleased to meet you."

The young reverend squinted at Tom with a quirky smile on his long face.

"Luke. Really? You don't look the type."

"Well, neither do you, to be honest."

"Not dressed up for it tonight, though?"

"No, well, I had some cowgirl boots and a Stetson I was going to wear, but I decided against it."

Reverend Luke chuckled.

"I've not seen you around," Tom pursued. "Are you on a mission here or something?"

"Always on a mission! Just trying to do my bit to put a smile on people's faces."

Ha! I don't need Archie – I'm really good at making friends. I'm going to call him friend, so he knows we're friends. Stupid Archie.

"I tell you, friend, it's so good to find a kindred brother."

"Preach it!" Reverend Luke declared, raising a hand pentecostally.

"So where are you on the conservative/charismatic spectrum?" Tom asked.

"Well, certainly charismatic – don't know about conservative!" The young vicar burst out laughing and Tom laughed back.

"So are you doing a bit tonight, friend?"

"Yeah. Using 'I'm gonna live forever'."

"Ah, classic eternal life message. Well good luck, friend – I'll stand near the front and show my support."

Friend.

Later, as Reverend Luke did his stuff, Tom stood near the front and surmised that Luke's "stuff" wasn't as theologically sound as he had expected. Mainly because he was a stripper.

Tom had thought that Luke and he were cut from the same cloth, but there hung between them one major chasm of a difference – that Luke got paid to take his clothes off to dance music, and Tom didn't.

* * *

"How did you find that, honeybunny?" Rachel asked on the way home. She was humming the Macarena and clicking her fingers tipsily.

"Well now, let me see. I got kissed by a woman who isn't my wife, lied repeatedly to a stranger about my job, nearly died from starvation, and then made friends with a man whose cassock was seamless. So not great. You?"

"Well, it was just nice to be out of the house for an evening, I thought. It's been so hectic since we got here. Oh, and while you were watching the 'sermon', Angela gave her life to the Lord."

"What?" There was disbelief in Tom's question but, oddly, no joy.

"Great, isn't it? She's been having a terrible time at work and drinking a lot to block it out. We just got talking in the conservatory, I shared a bit of the Gospel, and she said she needed Jesus."

Tom drove the rest of the way home in silence. It had happened again.

Rachel had left the soirée with the knowledge that she'd changed someone's life, boogying them onto the dance floor of the greatest party imaginable; she was a Big Fisher of men, and had reeled in another catch. By contrast, the only thing Tom had caught at the party was the sweaty, seamless, Velcro smock of a sexy fetish vicar.

God help me. Seriously.

By the time they got home, Tom was feeling physically empty from minuscule bites of canapé, and emotionally empty from the indelible image of Luke's ecclesiastical hips gyrating six inches from his face.

He needed comfort food – but nothing made of meat. *Absolutely not meat.*

Rachel, boiling the kettle for a Horlicks, tried to feed Tom with words of comfort.

"Tom, it's not a competition, you know, all this community building. We're a team, the three of us, and there's no 'I' in team."

"No, but there is an 'I' in ice-cream, which is what I'm getting."

Tom opened the freezer and excavated a tub from its icy depths. Dusting the snowy residue off the lid, he read aloud the words: "Authentic Cornish Vanilla".

Bingo. Already he could sense his anguish freezing to death like the final image in Kubrick's *The Shining.*

I may not have any friends, but ice-cream is my friend.

He unsheathed his favourite spoon from the drawer, mobilised his Batmobile-shaped bowl from the cupboard, and prised open the tub of delicious creamy dessert… to discover frozen soup.

What fresh witchcraft is this?

He paced angrily into the living room, thunking the tub of arctic vegetables down in front of Rachel.

"What do you call this?" Tom's voice was as cold as ice. "I can't believe you'd be willing to sacrifice our love like this. It's an outrage!"

"It's carrot and coriander – I made extra."

"But why did you make extra? I don't even like soup – nobody likes soup."

"I like soup."

"Nobody likes soup! I've never once turned to you, famished, and asked if we had any leftover soup. And why have you put it in an ice-cream tub? Did I offend you a year ago, and you decided to play the long game with revenge, biding your time, knowing that eventually, one night, when I was peckish, you'd be able to ruin my evening?"

"Tom, calm down, please. I don't like the way you're talking to me. I have never taken revenge on you. What's the matter? Come and sit down."

Rachel ushered him into his lazy-boy chair and looked sweetly perplexed.

Tom stared at his legs, which were swinging petulantly at the knee, kicking at nothing and everything.

"Tell me what's wrong," Rachel said, propping him up with the same palliative tone she had used when Amy, as a toddler, would wake crying in the night.

"It's just… I think… I don't know; it just feels like I'm getting everything wrong."

"But that's not–"

"Not true? Rachel, what have I actually achieved? Seriously, I'm asking you a serious question – what have I achieved? Who have I actually told about Jesus? Nobody. He's just a swear word here."

"It's not all about well-defined conversions, Tom."

"Yes, it is! It is for me and it is for Harvey and the people at Jesus4All. And besides, everyone else has done all right – even Selina has a higher conversion rate than me, and she eats from the bin."

Rachel was stroking Tom's miscellaneously styled hair which, she noticed for the first time, was newly flecked with white interlopers. From her angle, his head was an aerial view of tiny waves breaking on a muddy brown sea.

"I'm sorry you're feeling like this, honeybunny."

"Why do you call me that, anyway? It's a silly name."

"I don't know. I can't remember. It's not the worst name

you've been called since we got here. Would you like some soup?"

"No, I wouldn't. Nobo—"

"—dy likes soup, yes, you've said." She smiled and came to sit on the arm of his lazy-boy, which threatened to topple, so she sat on the footrest.

"Look," she continued, "I actually think you're doing pretty well. This was never going to be easy; it's not like selling carpets. Maybe it can't just be about shifting units?"

"But I'm being paid to evangelise. If I'm not bringing people to the Lord, I'm not doing my job. Our future as a family depends on me doing better."

"I don't think—"

"It does, it does… Rachel, it does." Tom had both palms raised, simultaneously a sign of peace and a subconscious barricade for counter-arguments.

"I'm here to win souls, not friends… not that I've won many friends. But I had plenty of friends when we lived in a place where the tourism and murder rates weren't neck and neck."

Rachel chuckled. "That was a good joke."

"And also, no matter wh— what did you say?

She smiled. "I said that was a good joke. Murder and tourism rates being the same. Very funny… a good joke."

"Wait, do you really think that… you think I told… " The irrepressible smile which oozed from Tom's mouth covered his features like ice-cream across the face of a messy toddler.

Rachel put sprinkles on top.

"I'm sorry if I don't laugh at your jokes enough, honeybunny. Or if I trick you into thinking soup is ice-cream."

"You do do that – I caught you red-handed. You're like a culinary super-villain."

"Haha! Wow, you're on fire tonight with these good jokes."

"Am I? Am I really?"

Rachel's smile covered him like a double duvet on a December morning.

She knew exactly what she was doing here, and Tom knew that she knew. But it didn't matter. He needed it.

Rachel placed both her hands on her husband's cheeks and looked directly into his eyes.

"Tom, I love you. I think you're doing a grand job here. Both Amy and I are very proud of you. OK?"

"OK."

"And there's still plenty of time, you know? 'Do not overlook this one fact... that with the Lord one day is as a thousand years, and a thousand years as one day.' Remember?"

"Bible."

"From the Bible, that's right. But it's true, isn't it? It's not about our timing. And you're preaching at the café launch next week. Maybe that's what it's been building up to all along?"

Tom thanked her, told her she was right and that he loved her – that he really loved her.

Feeling wanted and slightly less despondent – but still famished – he took the thawing soup back into the kitchen.

I was silly to get so worked up over frozen soup.

With recalibrated hope, Tom took a large cake tin down from on top of the fridge, and opened it to find... a slightly smaller tin. He sloped back in to Rachel.

"Could you make me some soup, please?"

"Of course."

"And can you do that thing where you microwave it in such a way that most of the ice won't have broken down but it will still manage to be far too hot?"

"Whatever you like, my brave man."

"Thanks."

Chapter 11

Dunna Dunna Dunna Dunna Fatman

om was in his man-cave, deleting Harvey's messages from the answer machine. He had genuinely been absent for most of them, but had conveniently turned up Marvin Gaye during one such transmission. There was nothing that Harvey could say which would shift Tom's spiritual impasse, nor did Tom want to hear about "our man in Mercia" and the overflow of his rival's apostolic cup.

He had more immediate concerns.

Tom's gardening leave had finished, and it was time for him to return to Roundhouse Primary School and to re-unite with Jake, post-exodus. He looked across at Barney – whose gardening leave had not been revoked – slumped lifelessly under the poster of Jesus (played by Robert Powell).

Looks like I'm on my own today, buddy. Don't eat too many tea cakes while I'm gone.

Roundhouse wasn't a bad school, and there was some solace to be found in the fact that Amy was loving it, although her ease at integrating held up an unflattering mirror to Tom's own fortunes.

Mirror, mirror, on the wall… thank goodness she takes after her mum.

"I like school, Daddy," Amy informed Tom on the drive over there. "I like being in Purple Set. Purple is my fourth favourite colour after violet, mauve and erm… light purple."

"Oh, yes?"

Tom reflected that, in his day, the children were split into sets one and two, not arbitrary colours like Purple and Green. He understood that the school was just trying to be sensitive about not stigmatising the less talented kids, but wondered how, in practice, one could fail to give away the hierarchy when Purple Set were asked for an essay on pet care and Green Set were advised not to eat from the sandpit.

Tom kissed his daughter at the school gates, and she sped off to find Suki and jump head first into a new day of learning fun.

She even runs like Rachel.

Tom set a resolute course towards Jake's classroom, the plap-plap-plapping of his plimsolls a little slower, a little more pathetic, than usual. Jake, as it turned out, was the school's only member of Yellow Set.

The colour of a sunbeam. Or urine.

As Tom plap-plapped through the Memorial Hall he passed Kathy, who was talking to a dinner lady about healthier meal options.

"Good morning, Mr Hillingthwaite," she said, with well-rehearsed power-precision. The mischievous little girl behind the mask was nowhere to be seen.

"Good morning, ma'am," Tom replied, overdoing the formality. He wasn't trying to be flippant – he just felt a tad uncomfortable with the sudden emotional distance. He also bowed.

The population of Yellow Set was sitting outside his classroom on what Mrs Quinn would tell Tom was the "thinking chair". She had been lying in wait for Tom, and sidled out of her classroom on his arrival, beaming with friendly dislike.

"Ah, Mr Hellishwait."

"Hillingthwaite."

"Yes. Now, as you can see, Jake has been having a time-out. His behaviour has been less than satisfactory over the last few weeks – ever since your last session, in fact. Odd how someone brought in to help could actually make things worse." Her smile was like a stitched-up wound. She looked down at Jake on his chair, then down on Tom, who was slightly taller than her.

"You do make quite a pair, don't you?"

Neither Jake nor Tom assented.

She's trying to shame us both in front of the other. She's really f… lipping horrible.

Mrs Quinn continued, digesting every nuance of the scene with huge enjoyment. "Now, listen. We want to help you out, you see" – she revealed a folder from behind her back – "so we've put together an easy-to-follow programme for you to work through together. Quite simple: nothing emotional, nothing religious. Just basic exercises to pass the time in a professional manner. All right?"

Anyone could see that this wasn't about facilitating. This was about a scorned woman with a hellish axe to grind, but the axe was at head height and ready to drop with fury; one wrong move, and Mrs Penelope Quinn would ensure that Tom never set foot in the school again.

She knew about Kathy and Petefeast: she would play that trump card when she needed to. She held all the power, and she loved it.

Breathe, Tom. Take it like a man.

"Thank you, Mrs Quinn; that's very kind of you. C'mon, Jake."

Wordlessly, Jake shuffled into the airless nook that passed for their study space. Tom picked up Jake's "thinking chair" – only briefly thinking about swinging it full into Mrs Quinn's face – and followed the lad through.

"Deal with it," he heard her hiss as she closed the door.

Tom took a seat in the cubby hole and opened up the file… then closed it again and looked at Jake, his lower lip protruding caricaturistically.

"I'm sorry, Jake. I'm sorry for what happened last time. I treated you like a little boy, and that was wrong of me. It won't happen again, I promise. OK? You have my word. Right, let's open the file, shall we?"

Jake didn't respond verbally, either to Tom's apology or to the trite exercises in Mrs Quinn's folder. The two cowed little boys – one of them wearing the mask of a grown man – sat there saying little, in a stuffy cubby hole with all the silence of a man-cave.

* * *

At the end of the session, after Jake had scrape-scuff-scraped back into class in his Salvation Army trainers, Tom returned to his car via his signature plap-plapping, nodding civilly at Kathy as he passed a meeting she was helming.

There was no car-park-angel sighting this time – no providential portent of heavenly comfort – and so Tom sought alternative refuge in patisserie. Equidistant between Roundhouse and Tom's square house, a Christian-run bakery was doing a roaring trade. The more elementary names for Christian bakeries (Daily Bread, Bread of Heaven, etc.) had been overlooked in favour of something more left-field, and yet

Baguette Behind Me Satan was renowned for selling the best Danish pastries in all Bruton. Tom, frustrated by Jake's vow of silence, purchased four Danishes (one for him, one for Rachel, one for Anne, another one for him), and ferried them home to Hillingthwaite Manor and to the man-cave.

The poor lad just probably sees me as some mad monk figure.

Tom had been spending a lot more time alone in his man-cave recently, because it was the one place in Bruton where he felt within his depth. Rachel would usually leave him alone in there, although Selina liked to interlope and send the resident mice flying in terror.

The boxes of comics were still in there – though one of them had been emptied to store clandestine packs of Tunnock's tea cakes – but now the leather lazy-boy had moved there, too. Tom was stretched out on it, re-re-reading *The Killing Joke* by Alan Moore and Brian Bolland, when Rachel entered, announcing with up-plucked courage, "Tom, I've got two things to say."

Tom looked up from his comic, the leather of his chair scrunching expensively.

"Is either of those two things that you're leaving me?"

"Of course not."

"Good. Is either of them that you've brought me another Danish pastry?"

"No."

"Bad. Still, continue…"

Rachel's face was uncharacteristically drawn with angst. She looked so sheepish, an insomniac could have counted her face and been instantly cured.

"Tom," she continued, with ongoing sheepishness, "I think you should go on a diet."

Tom took a petulant bite of his Danish pastry, then set it down and looked at her sheepdogly. Rachel's comment was the first drip in what he expected would become a conversational downpour.

"I don't really know how to start this conversation, honeybunny."

"You've already started it. What you mean is, you don't know how to continue it."

"I've just noticed that you've started to put on a bit of weight."

Tom picked up his Danish from where it was resting on the convenient sill of his belly, took another bite, and blithely quipped, "What are you saying? Does my bum look big in this?"

"No… it's more that the rest of the world looks suddenly smaller."

"I don't think that's a very good joke," Tom retorted, hurt.

"I'm sorry. I'm trying to be light-hearted, but it is an issue. When you wore that pair of shorts the other day, it looked like you'd been shrink-wrapped. They left very little to the imagination – in fact I started imagining lots of other scenarios just to get the image out of my head."

"Rude."

"I know. I've said I'm sorry. Please don't take this as condemnation – but I'm genuinely concerned for your health."

Tom looked down at his belly, then at the surreptitious box of tea cakes in the corner, then at Rachel.

"Yes, OK. I concede that I've been gorging a teensy bit to escape reality. I'll try to cut down. But why are you bringing this up now? Are you suddenly embarrassed to be seen with me?"

"Not because of what you look like, no." She attempted a smile, but it was the smile of a pilot bracing for impact. Something – some confession – was coming in to land.

"This isn't about image, honey. I'll love you no matter how big you get. God sees the inside – although he's probably had to

147

switch to widescreen at the moment." The undercarriage was being deployed.

"Then why is this suddenly so urgent for you?"

There was a pause, during which the seatbelt signs flashed madly, and after which Rachel whispered: "I'm pregnant."

Chapter 12

You Can Call Me "Joker"

It was the day of the community café launch.

This was the day: the day when Tom would finally get the chance to tell his neighbours and friend about Jesus.

To date, his greatest achievement in Bruton had been a one-man crusade to stop the word "Tomfoolery" slipping out of circulation, but the conversational dead ends, roadblocks and diversions would all be worth it if, today, Tom got to drive a message of salvation straight into the lock-up of people's hearts. He wasn't joyful, or excited, or looking forward to it. He was simply ready, spiritually armed, his loins girded.

The community café had been loosely operational for a few weeks, but this was the official launch to really put it on the local map. A name for the café had been chosen and, as Tom arrived that day, Rachel was tying a freshly unfurled banner to the gate. She had politely declined her husband's naming suggestions of Tea Total, Lord Teasus and Mr Tea, and had decided to call it "Café on the Corner". This made sense both alliteratively and geographically but, Tom would argue, had left very little room for celebrity patronage.

He observed her banner maintenance with husbandly care, stroking her head with patronising benediction. "Please be careful, Rachel. I don't want you overdoing anything in your condition."

"Ok, honeybunny. I'll try not to tie this piece of hemp too tight in case I break a sweat."

In spite of everything else going on, Tom was both joyful and excited about having another child. He wasn't ready, or spiritually armed, and his ungirded loins had been integral to the situation. But when the palpitations and night terrors (specifically, of fully grown babies screaming for Daddy) subsided, he could honestly say that he was looking forward to being a father again – although it did mean that the pressure to succeed in this job was now even greater, with Amy still fifteen years shy of being a barrister.

My yoke has been easier, that's for sure.

Café on the Corner was being launched with a comedy night and bonfire. Bruton wasn't known for its cultural output: a camp man walking down the street whistling would have been heralded as a full-on Mardi Gras, while the town's inhabitants tended to laugh at odd things, such as other people's suffering. A night of actual comedy then would be something a bit different, and would hopefully, Tom hoped hopefully, act as a flaming beacon on a winter's night, drawing people in from the freezing artistic extremities of the local environs – in which even using the word "environs" could get one set alight like a flaming beacon.

After the comedy, if the weather held, everyone would mosey out back and stand around the bonfire, toasting marshmallows.

The event looked set to be packed. Flyers and posters had been designed (by Rachel), sent to the printers (by Rachel), and collected (by Tom).

"I can do without the banner saying Café on the Karl Marx," Rachel had joked in all seriousness.

In addition to the blanket leafleting that Rachel and her "gals" from the weekly prayer hub had undertaken, Tom had personally invited all the Beetle Drivers from Bruton Pentecostal Church, to decisively show-not-tell them what a "relevant" event looked like. He witnessed them all descending on the venue in a wobbly fashion, extras from Night of the Not-Quite-Living-Nearly-Dead. Martin Hartnett, head of the Secular Humanist Society and Tom's only friend, pulled up shortly after them.

"Thanks so much for coming, Martin!"

"My pleasure, Tom. Congratulations on putting on a decent event."

It was all my wife's work, Tom didn't say. He led Martin inside, slaloming past Beetle Drive Merlin who was standing in the lobby, worrying that he'd left his house unlocked.

Inside the venue, Amy and Suki were decorating the tables with crisps and candles. The candles were those you might encounter at a séance, and Tom prayed that Babs wouldn't turn up and start heckling the comedian by asking if Derek was backstage.

A lot of Tom's invitees had asked whether it was a "BYOB" event. Blisslessly ignorant of what that meant but desiring, above all things, to stem the current of social unpluggedness that surged from him, Tom had told them all that yes, it was. When he discovered that BYOB meant "Bring Your Own Booze" and wasn't just slang for "good', it frazzled him – and not just because he had wished Rachel "BYOB luck" earlier in the day.

But BYOB has exactly the same number of syllables as "Bring Your Own Booze". What possible gain can there be in shortening it like that?

As it was, Tom Hillingthwaite had opened an accidental bar to a load of avid drinkers at a venue that demanded, in order to survive, the purchase and consumption of non-alcoholic drinks. As show time approached, Rachel was overwhelmed to see so many people filtering through the doors of the café, but underwhelmed that almost nobody was ordering tea or coffee.

"Who said they could bring alcohol?" she asked her husband.

"They must have thought it was a BYOB event," he offered by way of conciliation. Contrastingly, Tom had swallowed a lot of coffee, but the money he was spending came out of a joint marital bank account – the same bank account from which Rachel paid for all the coffee.

The really BYOB news was that almost all of Dews Close had turned up. Wayne the Tattooligan was there, fending off the autumn chill with an extra sleeveless vest, cuddling a twenty-four-pack of cheap stubby French beers (which British people take to all social events, where the beers draw inevitable comparisons with horse wee). Wayne's army of reprobate children, whose ranks seemed to have swelled further, were also there, playing a modified game of tag whereby you didn't just tag your sibling, but pinned them down and punched them repeatedly below the midriff.

"They gotta learn sometime, ain't they," Wayne shrugged, clocking Tom's contorted smile.

"What are they learning? That people in cafés are going to strike you in the privates?" Tom asked, rather boldly.

"Life hits you where it hurts when you don't expect it."

With a chilly sensation down his spine, Tom realised that Wayne was absolutely right, and left him to his philosophical meanderings and his crate of watery Gallic beer.

The man coming to entertain the masses that evening was a comedian called Victor Smithers. Tom had never heard of him, but then Tom's idea of a comedian was J. John.

Smithers was supposed to have arrived by now, but hadn't, so Tom sent him a text message: "U nrly hr fell0? xxx"

Tom hated the idea of text speak, but he was rushed off his

feet and it saved him valuable Martin-time, so he graciously absolved himself on this occasion.

Across the tastefully decorated café, maintaining a safe distance from Tom at all times, Catrina and Not-Carl had arrived and were mingling, Catrina asking other Dews Closians whether they had spotted her albino rabbit Mitsy, who had apparently made a break for freedom earlier that day. Tom (or Peeping Tom, as they had covertly nicknamed him) waved cordially, and they cursorily returned the gesture.

"No comedian yet?" Catrina asked politely.

"Not yet. I've just sexted him."

"Right."

Not being a fully fledged member of Generation Text, Tom didn't know that "sexting" wasn't merely "saying something in text speak". Nor did he know that he had, in fact, practically sexted Victor Smithers.

Catrina and Not-Carl went outside for a cigarette, which was curious only in that neither of them smoked.

The event was due to start at 7.00 p.m., but at 6.50 p.m. the comedian still hadn't arrived. Tom was outside, simultaneously keeping an eye out while trying to rebuke the oncoming rain clouds that threatened to saturate the bonfire; he had constructed it himself out of old pallets and random planks of wood, and it was structurally perfect.

BYOB – Build Your Own Bonfire. That would make more sense.

"Is there anything we can do to help?" a voice came from just inside the doorway. Standing there, framed in the interior glow, were Kathy and Jake.

A hundred contrasting sensations blitzed together inside Tom to form a veritable emotional smoothie.

"What… how… are you… hi," he managed.

"Hi, Tom," said Kathy softly, without a hint of power-play. "I hope you don't mind the two of us turning up?"

"No, it's… I wasn't… finetastic. Hi, Jake."

"Hi," Jake nearly said.

"Jake, why don't you go and find us somewhere to sit?"

Jake scuff-scraped back inside. Kathy moved closer in, her back to the door.

"What are you doing here, Kathy?"

"I'll tell you. But first of all, Tom, I'm sorry. I don't want to say much more than that, but I'm sorry." Her eyes – the eyes of a sad little girl, the eyes behind the mask – were sparklingly moist.

"Thank you. I'm sorry, too – I've been a complete shambles since I entered your school. You must think it's like having the ten plagues of Egypt all at once – you get rid of the frogs and the lice, turn round and your firstborn's dead."

"How much coffee have you had, Tom?"

"Plenty, thanks."

Kathy laughed a laugh of palpable affection. Then she lowered her head, her hands clasped in front of her in subconscious supplication.

"Tom, my position at Roundhouse is precarious, to say the least. Mrs Quinn has me where she wants me, and she'll strike out if she doesn't get her own way. I'm sorry, but I can't protect you from any of the bile that she throws at you, for fear that I'll lose my job."

Tom nodded grimly. "I understand that."

Kathy's tone brightened. "So I've gone external. She doesn't track my movements outside school – at least I don't think so! If the mountain won't go to Mohammed, eh?"

Tom knew this wasn't the time to challenge or debate the veracity of Islam, so he smiled and asked, "How did you bring Jake, though?"

"I rang his home. His poor mum has some substance issues which she's dealing with, so she's not always the most attentive, but she loves him very much. She said she was happy for me to bring him here. And I thought it might be good for him to see you on neutral ground."

Tom grunted ruefully.

"As I said to you before, Tom, I would love you to break through with Jake. It's the one area where Mrs Quinn is vulnerable. She can't teach him – she's got nothing – and the idea of someone being able to would drive her mad."

Suddenly it was back. Only briefly, but the mischievous grin of that little girl was back, and when it subsided the worried, hopeful face before Tom was not the domineering head of an urban primary, but the preacherman's daughter.

"I don't know," she finished. "I suppose I thought Jake might help us both find some redemption out of this."

Tom wanted to hug her. He didn't, though. Instead he said "Yes," and then, as he had now done three times with Kathy, he bowed.

Kathy nodded appreciatively at the bonfire, and went inside to get warm and caffeinated.

* * *

At 7.12 p.m. the comedian finally arrived.

"Did you find us OK?" Tom asked as he hurried the joker inside, buffeting him with a shard of rotting pallet.

"No, I didn't find you OK, fella. I'm still driving around the backstreets, lost – I'm planning on giving you a bell in a bit so you can guide me in."

Victor Smithers was in his mid-thirties, with overly gelled spiky black hair. Tom was taken aback by his cruel tone, but was too relieved he was there at all to quibble too much.

"Is there a green room?" Smithers asked tersely.

There wasn't a green room.

"Erm… yes." Tom took Smithers to the only closed-off area that wasn't being used for the event.

"This is the green room?"

"Erm… yes."

"It's a lift."

"It'll have to do, I'm afraid. I'm Tom, by the way."

"There's a mike though, yeah?"

"Erm… not sure… there's a Wayne, a Martin…"

"Is there a microphone?"

"Oh, I see – a microphone! No, there isn't a microphone. Can you just talk louder?"

"Well, yeah, if you want it to feel like a hostage situation?" The man's sarcasm almost imploded into a genuine question.

I don't want it to feel like a hostage situation – why would I? Why would anyone want the opening of a café to feel like a hostage situation?

But they didn't have a microphone and it was time to start the event.

"And you know it's a family show, so we need family-friendly material?"

"Yep, your missus told me all this on the phone. Leave it with me."

Tom took to the stage, which was more of a laminate floor (easier to flog than eternal life) and surveyed the expectant crowd in front of him. He asked everybody to take their seats and, where appropriate, to stop slamming each other in the testicles. Beetle Drive Merlin had Beetledriven home to re-lock his door, but the singular lack of empty seats was testament to all the faith and good works invested in the event.

Tom had prepared a few *bons mots* to warm up the audience, including a couple of jokes that he had downloaded from the internet; he would save the Gospel message for the end of the show. He was nervous, of course, but this was a chance to show a lighter, less creepy side than the one most of his neighbours had downloaded into their mental hard drives. Rachel had helped him rehearse, in that she had told him not to tell any jokes and just introduce the comedian. He had chosen to ignore his chosen on this occasion.

He began. "Thanks so much for coming to this café launch – we hope you're going to have a great time tonight, good evening!" The applause that he was expecting, and that one normally received at this sort of event, failed to materialise – possibly, he later reflected, because he had put "good evening" in completely the wrong place in the sentence.

"Now, some of you – all of you who don't share my surname, in fact – have BYOBed, and without wanting to make a big deal of that, we do also have some lovely, lovely coffee on sale at the counter. So if you could BYOBBDDI – bring your own booze but don't drink it… " He waited for the laugh… nothing.

"Well, as I say, there's coffee available." His left leg was starting to twitch anxiously at the frosty reception. It was OK, though – he still had his pre-prepared jokes to fall back on.

"And now, to mark this celebration, we have a comedian for your ears to delight upon. He's never been to Bruton before, and I know what that's like, oh, yes, let me tell you. On my first day here, I needed directions somewhere, so I asked if there was a Homebase, and the woman said, 'No, there's a B but no Q.'"

Amy, and only Amy, laughed.

"You said Homebase, honeybunny," Rachel pointed out, breaking the surprisingly loud silence.

"Sorry?"

"The joke is, 'Is there a B&Q?' but you said Homebase. It doesn't work as well. Or at all." Rachel seemed to be smiling, but it could have been that she was gritting her teeth very tightly.

Yes, it's that. She's not smiling at all.

"Oh, right, sorry. Suppose I should stick to the day job."

"Whatever that is," chimed Wayne the Tattooligan, who got a big laugh from everyone except Amy.

Tom tried to stagger on regardless, ignoring the throat-slitting "abort" gesture that his wife was making.

The show must go on.

"There's a lady down here called Anne. How much do you weigh?"

"I beg your pardon?"

"Oh, I can see you don't want to tell me – it's rude to ask a woman her weight. How about a different question then – how old are you?"

"I beg your pardon?" Anne said again, with exactly the same balance of emphasis and distaste.

"Wrong way round, Tom," Rachel interjected.

"What's the wrong way round?"

"You're supposed to ask the age and then the weight. It looks like a joke that way, and not just a series of increasingly personal questions. Sorry, Anne."

The jokes that Tom had fallen back on had turned out to be Samurai swords disguised as jokes.

"Quit while you're a head-case!" Wayne boomed.

"Bring on the comedian!" shouted Beetle Drive Lancelot.

"Fix the sewers!" shrieked the eau-de-toiletted lady from No. 1.

The rapturous clapping which greeted Victor Smithers' introduction was boosted by the sheer relief that Tom had stopped talking.

"If it wasn't for his personality, he'd be OK," Not-Carl whispered to Catrina, who was Googling "symptoms of Asperger's".

Beetle Drive Gawain had fallen asleep.

The generous applause built, crescendoed, and then petered out when everyone realised that the green room lift had disappeared and was currently languishing in the basement.

Oh dear. Should I do another joke?

"No," clipped Rachel, reading his mind.

Eventually, after a lot of graunching lift sounds, the metallic "Doors Opening" voice rang out and the comedian re-materialised. Tom flourished a hand of welcome in Smithers' direction and took a seat next to Amy and Rachel.

"You're funny, Daddy," Amy told him.

"I love you anyway," added Rachel, her teeth now un-gritted.

"Hello, I'm Victor. Sorry I'm late – the toilet downstairs was a bit murky."

There isn't a toilet downstairs, Tom and Rachel thought in unison.

"Deal with it later," Rachel lisped through re-gritted teeth.

"Just out of interest," Smithers smirked, "is there a Homebase in Bruton?"

Most of the audience collapsed into fits of laughter – Martin actually snorted.

I should surely take some of the credit – I set him up for that.

Smithers was ebullient. "What a guy, huh? You know, he sent me three kisses in a text."

Rachel skewed Tom a sideways glance.

I didn't.

"I didn't, I didn't," he whispered dismissively.

"Anyway," Smithers continued, "I've got another question. How do you take a very small penis and increase it to ten times the size? It's not a joke – can anyone help me with that?"

Oh no oh no oh no oh no.

The time to laugh had come and gone in record time. Even Wayne, who seemed quite happy to let his army of kids pummel each other in the nether regions, baulked at the poor taste. Rachel's gritted teeth were now airtight, her hands over Amy's ears, whose hands were over Suki's ears.

"Look," said Smithers, "I know it's a clean gig, so I've replaced the word I'd normally use there. It's fine. Anyway, I was having intercourse with my girlfriend…"

"Oh, goodness me!" exclaimed Beetle Drive Guinevere, damselly.

"It's not rude!" the comedian protested.

"It's not suitable for children!" Amy barked.

"I bet he's racist as well," the lady from No. 1 exclaimed.

"This guy said it would be OK," Smithers protested, pinpointing Tom with a rigid digit.

A roomful of heads ticked over to Tom like clock hands striking midnight.

I didn't.

"I didn't… I di… " he tailed off.

The ensuing silence was deafening. Smithers eventually smashed it.

"Oh, look, I'm off! I'm sick of gigs like this." The performer stormed offstage and back to the lift. His defiant exit was made more protracted when he accidentally sent himself to the first floor and had to come back down via the stairs. Several handfuls of punters bustled off after him, their evenings curtailed, expletives dropping from their mouths like litter.

* * *

Tom stared abjectly at the evaporating sea of faces in front of him. At Wayne, at Anne, at Catrina, at Kathy. At Jake and Amy. He saw in every single face his multitude of sins reflected back. And he knew it was over.

"Would you excuse me momentarily?" he said quietly, his incongruous middle-classness terminally on show.

He followed the baying, fraying crowd out of the venue into the advancing dusk. The joker's tail lights blinked angrily at him from down the street. It was pouring down now, the wood of the bonfire soaked through with mindless, slanting rain. Tom had no coat, but he couldn't be inside any more.

The remorseless downpour battered his face and penetrated his clothes as Tom Hillingthwaite crumpled onto the wooden pyre: just one more wet plank who couldn't start a fire if he tried.

And I have tried. Have I not tried? Father, I've tried…

He *had* tried in Bruton. He really had. And now he was crying in Bruton, and properly; the heavens opened behind his eyes and a warm deluge fell.

I can't do it…

"I can't do it… I CAN'T BLOODY DO IT, ALL RIGHT?"

The sheeting rain grasped his words and slammed them back into the ground. Who was he shouting at, anyway? God? The people of Bruton? Someone else?

He wasn't sure.

Where was that angel now, when he needed him? What was the point of an angel who didn't help – who didn't actually do anything?

"I can't do it, Father… Where are you? I need you, Father, please…

"Dad, I need you. I can't do it any more…

"Please… Father, I can't do it…

"Where are you, Dad?"

His words deteriorated into sobs.

This was supposed to have been the day when the wonderful message of Jesus reached the people of Bruton – the day when Tom could stand and proudly watch as a line of souls filed into the Kingdom of God. But he had failed again. He hadn't even got to talk about Jesus; his sales figures were like his bank balance: zero.

And what would they see in him, anyway? What was there about him that would encourage someone – anyone – to become a Christian? He was just a parochial carpet salesman who'd had the rug pulled from beneath his feet; whose hope had prematurely worn out.

"I'm just a little boy… I'm just a stupid little boy!"

His clenched fist smashed into the implacable concrete floor.

Tom sat foetally for ten minutes beneath the unyielding rain, silently beseeching it to wash away the shame. He was too numb to notice the music and singing that had bubbled up inside the building.

"Daddy? Daaaadddyyy?" It was Amy's voice.

Her smiling head peered round the door, light pouring out from the café. Tom barely looked up.

"Daddy, come and join in – it's very fun!"

Amy cantered out into the downpour, grabbed Tom by the arm and tugged until he stood up. She didn't ask him if he was crying, or mention the fact that his clothes were heavy with rainwater. She didn't mind about either – he was her daddy.

Sluggishly, grudgingly, his groanings too deep for words, Tom rose to his feet and followed his daughter's footsteps back into the café.

And found people having fun.

The whole crowd (those who hadn't left in the post-Smithers walk-out) were singing and clapping along to Wayne the Tattooligan's rendition of "A Little Less Conversation". People were laughing and waving their hands, while the tables had been stacked to one side to make space for a dance floor, on which Catrina and Anne were foxtrotting and Martin had broken out the robot.

Wayne was actually a surprisingly good singer, although his Elvis-style arm-wheeling and knee-trembling looked uncannily as though someone had tasered him. Nevertheless, he followed up his tribute to the King with a medley of Roy Orbison, Bruce Springsteen and Whigfield.

Tom Hillingthwaite stood on the margins and watched the people of his neighbourhood do-si-do-ing themselves into a community.

And then he saw something that he had never seen before: he saw Jake smile.

Not at Tom, and not because of anything Tom had done. But Wayne, after a grotesque attempt at the "didi-dadadaa" that concludes "Saturday Night", effortlessly hoisted the young lad onto his shoulders and started doing a conga. In customary obedience, the revellers hooked on to the end and jigged around the room in one joyful, unified chain.

And Jake grinned. And he grinned and he grinned.

And Tom grinned, too.

* * *

Later on, as the clouds and the guests parted, Tom stood in the darkened lift and watched a ticker-tape of happy customers thank Rachel for such a top evening.

Wayne and Anne linked arms as they left, sharing stories of Graceland and Elvis. The Tattooligan's kids and Amy made unfeasible plans to be best friends forever, the mixture of tiredness and e-numbers doing for infants what Jägermeister does for students.

The Beetle Drivers of the Round Table chuntered cheerfully as they ambulated home, and even Guinevere – whose new hip had briefly popped out during the conga – said it was the most fun she'd had in an epoch.

Rachel hugged Kathy as the preacherman's daughter left the café, gently whispering something into Kathy's ear with a smile. Then Rachel handed Jake a bag of muffins for the road, and the head teacher chaperoned the lad back to her car. But not before she had turned to Tom in his shadowy enclave – and bowed.

"Coffee?" Rachel asked later, as she and Tom sat in the half-light of an empty café.

"No, thanks. I think I might need to cut down."

"Here, have this." Rachel had unfurled the emergency fire blanket from the wall, and now wrapped it round Tom's damp shoulders for warmth. "It suits you."

Everyone had gone. The place had been swept, the store cupboard which Smithers mistook for a toilet fumigated. Catrina had escorted Amy home and put her to bed, while Martin had taken the lady from No. 1 for a nightcap.

"Are you OK?" Rachel asked, massaging her husband's shoulders beneath the blanket.

Tom gazed upwards at the foam ceiling tiles and gave his answer some serious thought.

"Yes," he said. "And I'm sorry."

His wife smiled down at him.

"I forgive you. I forgive you for putting too much pressure on yourself… for acting like a lone wolf… for trying to flog Jesus on sale or return."

Tom chuckled wryly at the retail analogy, then yelped when she karate-chopped his neck in mock punishment.

"And hey, I know the outcome of this event wasn't what you hoped for… but what happened here tonight was incredible. Everyone we know came together and had a great time."

Rachel paused to let her husband fire back with reasons why that wasn't good enough; why it was all about bums on seats in the Kingdom. But he didn't. He just nodded.

Rachel continued, "Tom, I know that you want to see people meeting Jesus – that you want them to get it like we got it; I know that, honeybunny. But this one-man crusade stuff doesn't work. People becoming Christians is between them and Jesus. Maybe all we can do – maybe all we need to do – is just show them that we care? And we did that tonight. We tried to give them a good evening, and they had it."

"I know."

"Good, I'm glad you know, because it's true. Your job title is Community Builder, and what you did tonight has helped to build community. You did your job really well. So let's do some more of that, shall we?"

The mischievous grin that split Tom's face drew a resolute line across his past.

"Let's do some more of that," he agreed. "Let's do lots more of that."

Tom Hillingthwaite stood up from his chair. And with his fire-blanket cape swooshing behind him, he went out into the night.

Chapter 13

The Breakfast Club

The weather outside was frightful, but inside Hillingthwaite Manor Tom and Rachel were settling down to watch *The Dark Knight Rises*, having worked together on a new plan of action for the next community event: a Family Fun Day.

It would be held to show love not just to the people of the surrounding streets, but to the wider community – and would be there to bless, not mess; to reach out, but not teach about. Dews Close had been a sort of pastoral training pool, and now the tentacles of community would stretch out into the wider town, with the two Hillingthwaite adults having equal control.

As Tom was ferreting around for the DVD remote and Rachel was noting down, "Forbid Tom from dressing as clown" on an A4 planning pad, the land line rang for the umpteenth time that week.

"W.T.Flip – it'd better not be that prank caller again!" Tom puffed.

The family were getting tired of the anonymous, silent calls. When they first arrived in Wessex only Tom had been on the receiving end, and in his insecure state he had started to worry that people found his voice so instantly infuriating that they couldn't bear to hear another syllable. Consequently, he had started road-testing various foreign accents when answering the phone.

But then it had begun happening to Rachel as well, and so they had written the calls off as sales guff. This pleased Rachel because, while Tom's French accent was charming, his Bavarian was on the wrong side of Third-Reichy and his generic West African raised all manner of questions – the answer to most of which was "No".

Just recently the frequency of calls had increased, and so it was with suitably attenuated hopes that Tom answered the DVD remote (which was lying by the phone) and then the actual phone.

"Aloha?" he asked, in passable Hawaiian.

"Hello, is that Tom?" The man on the line sounded weary.

"Yes."

"Hi there, Tom. It's Bill here from the Lamb and Flag Cossacks – remember?"

"Bill! Yes, of course. Aloha! Hello, I mean."

"Yes. Look, I won't keep you, but we've got a cup game tomorrow and we've got a load of injuries. I don't suppose…" Bill sounded hesitant. "I don't suppose you could come and make up the substitutes?"

Make up the…

Tom jumped up and started dancing like a hula girl. He couldn't decide whether to say "Suretainly" or "Finetastic", so instead he just smiled at the phone.

"Tom, are you there? You haven't fainted, have you?"

"No, here I am, Lord – Bill, I mean. And yes, I can play. I'd love to play. I never thought I'd play in the FA Cup!"

"It's not the FA Cup, Tom. It's the Southern Pub League Association Cup, sponsored by Mick's Abattoir. Look, if you can't make it…"

"No, I can definitely make it, Bill! Definitely can I make it. I didn't know there was more than one cup, but I'll be there!"

"Good. Bring a towel this time."

Bill told Tom the time and the place and rang off. Tom's hula dance evolved into a conga, and he clumped round the living room singing "Play, football, play" to the tune of "Shine, Jesus, Shine".

Rachel asked Tom to sing in his own voice rather than generic West African, but then she joined the two-person conga and they shimmied their way round the house – the Hillingthwaites alive with the sound of music.

Because everyone deserves a second chance.

* * *

The morning of the big match arrived, and by the time Rachel and Amy had come downstairs for breakfast, Tom was dressed in full "soccerman" attire and doing some shadow-boxing that he'd picked up from the training session.

"I thought you were going to play football," Rachel said as she poured Amy some cereal. "Are you expecting much hand-to-hand combat?"

"I'm just warming up, my chosen. You wouldn't understand."

Tom had been studying the moves of the Kung-Fu Gardener, and had adapted his signature jab, jab, swear-loudly-at-the-bin technique into a simple jab, jab, don't-swear-at-all.

"Daddy, you look like a lady."

"No I don't, my love. That's quite rude… Van Damme, Van Damme."

"Your daughter is quite correct, actually," Rachel responded. "It's the headband, I think. Is that part of the official kit, may I ask? And when will I get it back?"

"Well, to answer the first bit, no, but it just gives me a certain *je ne sais quoi*. And in answer to your second question," Tom answered, bicep-curling a rolling pin, "as soon as I get back."

Rachel slotted two pieces of toast under the grill, then handed Tom a pair of football boots that she had pre-emptively borrowed from Not-Carl.

"I didn't want you losing a shoe again, and I don't think white plimsolls will cut it in a competitive match."

"Wow, that's so kind of him. How can I thank them, do you think?"

"I think by just cleaning them, then leaving them silently on the doorstep in a bag. I think they'd really appreciate that."

Tom nodded, then returned to his domestic warm-up. Setting his legs shoulder-width apart, he thrust down to touch his toes – and came back up retching.

* * *

Tom drove to the Kris Akabusi Sports Centre, psyching himself up by listening to Marvin Gaye's "How sweet it is to be loved by you", replacing the words "loved by you" with the words "playing in a football match". It didn't scan very well, but the headband was playing havoc with his circulation.

He arrived at the ground and located Bill. In accordance with his genus, the boss was carrying a bag of balls and wearing a sheepskin jacket. He pointed Tom towards the changing rooms and ordered him to remove the headband.

"We don't need another Steve Foster, thanks," Bill snorted. The Steve Foster to whom Bill was referring was an eccentric headband-sporting defender who used to play for Luton Town in the 1980s. It was also, however, the name of a lad who went to school with Tom and was expelled for slaughtering all the fish in the pond. Tom agreed that they didn't need another Steve Foster, but found it odd that Bill should bring that up now. The headband was starting to leave a red mark anyway, so he took it off and put it away.

"I've brought my own kit today, Bill," Tom boasted, "so I can save you a bit of laundry."

What Tom was referring to by "my own kit" was a tee shirt of roughly the same brown as the Cossacks' strip, on the back of which he had painted the name "Anointed" and the number 1.

Bill the Boss thought seriously about forfeiting the tie.

When he made his way out onto the pitch to warm up (now wearing the regulation kit), Tom recognised a lot of the other lads from his unsuccessful footballing "audition". Dazza was there; in fact he appeared to be the captain. He clocked Tom's incoming star-jumps and came over to shake him forcefully by the hand.

"All right, geezer? Thanks for bailing us out. You ready?"

"Indeed. Let's 'ave it off!"

"It's 'Let's 'ave it'."

"Yes, of course."

"C'mon, then…"

Dazza got the lads warmed up, which entailed running after him from one side of the pitch to the other, slowly at first, but then quicker, sometimes stooping to touch the ground on the call of "Low", sometimes jumping to head an imaginary ball on the call of "High". Tom found it quite a fun game, and actually preferred it to football.

"Tom, you're the new boy. Call out 'High' and 'Low', yeah?"

"OK, then… wait for it… ready… Simon says 'High'!"

The entire Cossacks team erupted into laughter as they leapt into the air.

"Simon says 'Low'." The lads stooped to touch the ground, but there was still some tittering, which Tom was yet to understand.

"High!" Tom commanded, and the brown shirts jumped to

head the imaginary ball.

"A-ha, caught you out! Simon didn't say it!"

No one seemed to take any notice of the rules, and the lads who should really have sat out the next round through elimination just carried on with the warm-up.

Does Simon's authority hold no sway these days?

Shortly after that, the match kicked off. In their oddly brown kit (which the Dulux colour chart would have pinpointed as "hint of excreta") the Cossacks players rallied one another with esoteric cries of "Get ya 'eads on early doors" and "Smash their faces in!" Bill the Boss paced up and down the touchline in his ovine jacket, clapping his hands rousingly and shouting, "Come on, you Ruskies!"

On hearing the use of the Cossacks' unofficial nickname, Tom felt a pang of regret that he had so ruthlessly disposed of all his business cards.

Maybe I should get a new batch printed? They probably still have the proof.

From his place on the sidelines with the other subs Tom watched intently, shouting, "Come on, football!" and once, by accident, "Go, Score-inthians!"

As far as he could decipher, by the midway stage of the encounter it was one point per team, and it seemed to be going reasonably well – aside from Bill reprimanding Tom at one point, when one of the Cossacks players started limping, and Tom offered to swap with him for five minutes until he was feeling better.

"Tom, you can't go off and then come back on after you've been subbed – you know that, don't you?"

Well, I do now, yes – although it seems a little bit final. I mean, what if you just need to pop to the loo?

With ten minutes to go, Tom took advantage of being able to pop to the loo, and when he returned from the undergrowth

Bill and Dazza were waving frantically at him, as though guiding in a Boeing 737. Tom waved back and mouthed, "That feels better", then very quickly discovered through the medium of shouted curses that the Cossacks had conceded another point, and were now losing. Worse still, one of Tom's comrades was being stretchered off, while all the other understudies had already been used. They needed him to go on!

This is it. Time for Bill to unleash his beast, Tom thought ominously, still unaware of that phrase's full range of connotations.

"Shall I DM, Dazza?" Tom asked as he jogged nervously onto the pitch.

"No, mate, we're losing, so we need you to go and stay in defence while other lads push up. Just get the ball and hoof it up-field, OK? And stop star-jumping."

It was the first sentence that Tom had understood in its entirety all match, and he duly consented.

The remainder of the fixture was marked by a lot of tension and huge swathes of bad language, as Tom's team sought to score a much-coveted equaliser, without much luck. Tom stood gamely at the back but didn't really get the ball, given that most of the other players were camped in the opposing half. He kept himself focused and attuned by discreetly singing "Eye of the Tiger" – to the tune of "Be Thou My Vision".

Before long, Dazza was gesticulating again, signalling for Tom to come and join in the siege of the enemy goal. Apparently, they only had a few seconds left to score a point and everyone seemed a bit fractious.

Should I offer to pray?

Through a poor refereeing decision, deep into stoppage time the Lamb and Flag Cossacks were gifted a corner ball, and Dazza commanded Tom to go and make a nuisance of himself in the six-yard box. Tom galumphed forward – Not-Carl's boots a couple of sizes too big – and jockeyed for position in the other team's area, inadvertently standing on the opposition keeper's foot as he did so. He duly apologised but, by way of rejection, the goalkeeper pushed him moderately hard in the chest, sending Tom toppling backwards to the floor, his oversized boots flailing in the air. The referee's whistle split the air, and as he regained equilibrium Tom was keen to inform the adjudicator that treading on the keeper's foot was nothing more than an accident.

"I'm sorry, Mr Umpire, but these aren't my actual boo—" Abruptly, Dazza's hand clamped across Tom's mouth as he led him forcefully away.

"You've got us a penalty, mate. Well done and shut up."

"Mmm-hmm," Tom replied through Dazza's hand-vice.

Tom hovered outside the penalty area – other brown shirts winking chummily at him – and watched as Dazza kicked the ball straight into the goal from the penalty spot… and all of a sudden Tom found himself running after Dazza along with his team-mates, shamelessly taking part in the most mature, manly pile-on to which he had ever been privy. Again, he actually preferred it to the football.

Dazza was prostrate on the ground, other Cossacks climbing on top of him with jubilant curses.

"O.M.Gosh, that was a nice kick!" was Tom's contribution to the celebrations.

Before Tom even had chance to excavate himself from the hasty human pyramid, the final whistle blew and the Lamb and Flag Cossacks had forced a replay – Dazza's last-minute equaliser proving decisive.

"Well done, you Ruskies!" Bill the Boss whooped from the touchline.

"All games finish equal, but some are more equal than others," Tom quipped to one of his team-mates, who looked confused to the point of being upset.

As the two teams left the field, Tom approached the opposition keeper to enquire about the state of his toe. The goalie thanked Tom for his pastoral concern by telling him to be sexual in a wayward direction, and so Tom headed back to where Bill was gathering his comrades for a team talk. As his oversized boots clumped him over, bits of turf flying up everywhere, a deafening cheer erupted from Tom's huddled team-mates. Even Bill didn't look totally nonplussed by him for once.

"'Ere comes the real hero," Dazza hooted. Brazenly shirtless in posturing virility, Captain Fantastic patted Tom manfully on the back – which really stung.

"Well done, geezer," the fatherly leader snarled.

"Tom needs to play every week!" one of the lads declared.

"Hey, Simon didn't say it!" exclaimed another, and exultant laughter ascended skywards.

As at the training session, Tom politely refused to shower communally. Despite the obvious bonding that the day had facilitated, his views on recreating scenes from ancient Greece post-match hadn't changed, and the added level of celebratory intimacy made him more, not less, wary.

I'm not prudish, but also… I am.

Tom collected up his homemade replica shirt and headband, congratulating Bill the Boss on his tactical *nous* and guile.

"You know where I am if you need me, Bill."

"I do, Tom, I do. God forbid we ever need you again, but somehow you've saved us today, so thanks."

Tom was happy to overlook the theological inconsistencies in Bill's speech, deferring the opportunity to expound on the concept of salvation. He simply wished the boss well and went off in search of Dazza, beckoning the skipper to his red Sedan.

"Thanks once again for all your support, Dazza – I really enjoyed it today. And look, I brought you some of the tasty muffins from my wife's café. I hope you like them, O Captain, my Captain!"

Dazza, someone known for wearing his morals at a jaunty angle, had never been proffered fairy cakes in a sports-centre car park before. But he wasn't someone who often got given presents, and so he said, "Thanks." And then again, after jabbing Tom playfully and excruciatingly in the ribs, "Thanks."

Then went off inside the sports centre to gallivant naked with people of the same sex.

Tom made the drive home in record time, mentally hula-dancing all the way.

* * *

It was the next day, and Tom Hillingthwaite was once again orbiting Roundhouse Primary School, hoping to avoid getting burnt up on re-entry. Not just hoping, though: hopeful.

For the first time in weeks he felt free. The pressure – that untenable pressure to single-handedly save Wessex one West Saxon at a time – had gone. It had been ousted by a new regime: not simply to spread the Gospel, but to be the Gospel. The lone wolf had stopped hunting and was making his way back to the pack.

Tom's plimsolls plapped out their traditional plapping as he beat a path down the Dettol-reeking corridor, passing Mrs Quinn's class and furnishing her with a big, obedient smile as he did so. She did not reciprocate.

I know something you don't know, milady.

Jake, fresh from his debauched night out at a Christian-run community café, was already imprisoned in the spiderish cubby hole, popping air through his lips and tapping the desk in front of him.

"Hi, Jake," Tom said as he squeezed into the room.

Jake grunted. Tom took a seat next to him and opened his satchel.

"Jake, thanks so much for coming to the café launch. It was great to see you."

Jake grunted again.

"Could you pass me Mrs Quinn's file, please?"

Listlessly, Jake picked up the impeccably sheathed portfolio of basic exercises and handed it to Tom.

"Thank you, Jake. Now, let me see here…" Tom hurled the file at the window, sending papers skittering across the floor. "Whoops."

Jake looked up abruptly.

"Jake, today you can just relax and do your own thing. You don't need people telling you what to do all the time – least of all me."

Tom reached into his satchel and brought out a selection of comics that he'd purchased from the newsagents. "Take your pick, enjoy yourself – we don't have to have a conversation. Just don't tell Mrs Quinn, OK?"

Tom looked earnestly at Jake, who nodded. They spent the rest of the time in silence, Jake pawing through a Superman comic, Tom reading a collector's edition *Batman and Son* that he was already part-way through.

When the bell rattled the end of the lesson, Jake closed the cover of *Man of Steel* and handed it back to Tom.

"Keep it."

Jake grunted again and then carried his scrawny frame back into the corridor, past the "thinking chair", and back into Mrs Quinn's class, without another word.

Except for "Bye".

He said, "Bye."

And Tom Hillingthwaite punched the air.

Chapter 14

Dog Day Afternoon

*H*aving switched roles from Community Messer to Community Blesser, but having sworn on an actual Bible that he wouldn't use that motif with anyone except Rachel, the following week Tom popped round to see Wayne the Tattooligan, to ask if there were any acts of service he could perform. After all, Wayne had been responsible for the smile on Jake's face – and had almost single-handedly saved the comedy night from disaster – so Tom felt almost as emotionally indebted to his neighbour as he was fiscally indebted to the bank.

Almost.

One of Wayne's many despicably mannered minions led Tom into the lounge where the vest-clad lord of the manor was watching Sky Sports, propped up on the sofa by three large cushions, one of which was his own belly.

"Hi there, Wayneighbour…"

"All right." There was no hint of inflection in the voice. Wayne wasn't really asking if Tom was all right.

It was Tuesday afternoon, and so the televised sport was one of those which either nobody has heard of, or everyone has heard of and thinks is boring – hyped erroneously to attract people who won't sniff out the dullness beneath all the perfumed glitz and faux drama: people like Wayne.

Apparently, Wayne was watching the Fishomania World Series of Power Fishing. Or, as Tom would have called it, fishing. Keen to rebuild some of his sabotaged community bridges, however, Tom enquired whether Wayne enjoyed that sort of thing.

"That's why I'm watching it, mate."

An exciting moment in the fishing then caught Wayne's attention and he made a primal noise of incredulous appreciation. It looked very much to Tom as if someone had caught a fish with a fishing rod, but Wayne informed him, uninitiated as Tom was, that the catch was no ordinary marine life.

"He's Darkheart. Never been caught. They say he's cunning – pure evil!"

"Who says that?"

"Everyone in the business."

The business of telling porky pies, perhaps, but I didn't get where I am today by saying stuff like that out loud. Or rather I did, and I don't like where I am today – watching programmes where fish have their own back-story.

"Looks like a leviathan contest," Tom offered glibly.

"What sports are you into, then?" Wayne interrogated. "Bloody Classic FM?"

"It's more of a radio station than a sport… but yes, I like it. Though I take an active interest in lots of sports – Monopoly, Carcassonne, Risk… played golf once."

This was technically only a half-truth. Tom had once played crazy golf but, owing to a gang of belligerent wasps who kept pursuing Amy's ice-cream, he had ended up swinging the golf club in savage fatherly retribution while screaming, and was asked to leave the Children's Zone.

"Favourite golfer?" Wayne whistled blithely through his intermittent teeth.

"Oh, I don't think I have one… No, I like them all."

"You like them all?" Wayne responded, brutally mimicking Tom's middle-class tones.

"Yes."

"You like every single golfer?"

"Yes."

In truth, the only thing Tom knew about golf was that Tiger Woods sounded like an ill-fated National Trust property.

"I play for a football team!" Tom rejoined, feeling as though this conversation had all the cut and thrust of a gladiatorial game of Monopoly. He had turned over his chance card.

"Football, yeah? What position?"

"DM. It means defensive midfielder."

"I know what it means. You play for a team?"

"Well, I had an audition for one, and I played in a cup game for them – not the FA Cup, the other one?"

"League Cup?"

"I suppose it must have been…"

Wayne seemed genuinely interested, and turned his body towards Tom.

"Which team? Chelsea? Not Spurs?"

"The Lamb and Flag Cossacks."

Wayne re-hefted his body, his coating of tattoos pitching to and fro like primitive cinema, his gaze reverting to the indefatigable Darkheart.

Do not pass go. Do not collect £200.

"So… I was wondering, Wayne, erm, whether you had any jobs that needed doing that I could help with?"

"Lost your job, 'ave ya?"

"No, not at all. Not yet, anyway. I'm just wanting to do some stuff that helps out my neighbours."

"Great, so you'll be moving house then?"

"Oh, well…"

Wayne laughed raucously, sending tremors through his huge belly which, in turn, knocked another of the cushions to the floor.

"Joshing ya, mate. S'pose you could take the dog for a walk if ya wanted. I'm not leaving this seat while Darkheart's on the loose."

"The dog…?"

"Yeah, you've met him."

"Yes… I was thinking more that I could get you some shopping or wash your half-car or something."

"Well, tell ya what, let's start with the dog walk, and if ya do well, we'll look at getting ya onto some other stuff!" Wayne cackled. What Tom had thought might be his "Get out of jail" card looked set to be more like getting kicked in the head with an oversized boot or squashed with a novelty iron.

It wasn't that Tom didn't like dogs – far from it. Rather, having recovered Catrina's albino rabbit in the aftermath of the comedy night, he was reluctant to have dominion over local animals. (Mitsy the rabbit had been sheltering beneath the unused bonfire, which some local youths had set alight for a jape during the night. The next day, Tom had been sweeping away the ash and found what he initially thought to be a discarded kebab. He hadn't yet had the heart – or the stomach – to tell Catrina, and had secretly buried Mitsy in the back garden, wrapping her in his "Live every day like it's nice but you can probably expect to live for another 30 to 40 years" tee shirt.)

The walk to the Alvin Stardust Community Park was harrowing, with Wayne's dog – a boisterous bullmastiff – making regular attempts to slip his lead and make sweet canine love to anything sentient. When they arrived at the green belt, Tom tried to talk firmly to the dog, explaining in a tempered but logical manner that, while he wasn't against the creature having fun, there was to be no running off.

Dogs respond well to an authoritative voice.

Rearing and rolling, the dog slipped his collar and bounded off in search of play.

Even animals sense my lack of authority.

Ten minutes later, Tom had seen neither head nor tail of the beast and was starting to get worried – worried that he would have to trudge back to the Tattooligan's house and explain that, as a Wayneighbourly gesture, he had released the man's pride and joy into the wild. He was also wondering how Noah managed with two of every breed when, for Tom, retrieving a single dog was like herding cats.

Keen to maintain the physical relationship between his head and his body, Tom needed to locate the mongrel – and fast. Consequently, and totally in conflict with how he had expected his life to look in his mid-thirties, Tom Hillingthwaite found himself standing on his own, in a park, shouting at the top of his voice, "BOOBIES?... BOOBIES!... BOOBIES, HERE, NOW!"

The dog failed to return, but a man in a trench-coat crept out of a nearby bush looking hopeful.

Dejected, frightened, and preparing to cringe at the revelation of Boobies' moving back-story, Tom made the walk of shame back to Wayne's house, prophesying that the empty lead in his hand would come in very handy as a noose for his inevitable demise.

He was about to turn disconsolately back into Dews Close, prayers of penitence and faith heralding his coming, when Selina the cat flew past him at full pace, followed slobberingly by a lunatic bullmastiff: Boobies. In a less cathartic version of *The Incredible Journey*, the dog had presumably chased a series of increasingly large and fast creatures – starting with a vole and culminating in Selina – and somehow made his improbable way home. Tom shivered at the thought that Boobies must have crossed about eight roads in rush-hour traffic, but it occurred to him that such a concept would make a pretty good programme for midweek Sky Sports.

The main thing was that the dog hadn't perished, and nor would Tom.

And that really is the most I could have hoped for out of this.

Giving up the chase once Selina took up a position of safety on the Kung-Fu Gardener's shed, Boobies lolled happily back towards his lair, Tom hastily tagging along to make it look as though he hadn't made a pig's ear out of a dog's walk.

Meanwhile, back at the Fishomania World Series of Power Fishing, the indomitable Darkheart had finally been domitabled, and was now hanging lifeless from a weighing hook. But for a providential spot of luck, Tom might well have suffered the same fate, but as it was he had slipperily evaded catastrophe. It was the first time a situation had ravelled out of chaos.

You can call me Lightheart.

Tom "Lightheart" Hillingthwaite made the short walk back to No. 3, doffing an imaginary cap to the winner of the "Dog with the World's Most Crass Name" competition, mentally collating a list of possible candidates for "The Show where Animals Chase Other Animals in a Roughly Ascending Order".

Who teaches us more than the beasts of the earth?

It was another job well done.

* * *

That evening, after a dinner of liquid vegetables masquerading as ice-cream, the Hillingthwaites were sitting in their family room, reflecting on a good day's work all round. By this stage in their incumbency, the resident damp that had begun as a torrid, afflicting assault on the nostrils was now something of an old friend – an old friend, albeit, who smelt harrowingly of damp.

Tom had lugged the lazy-boy chair back from his man-cave, and the space was currently being put to good use as a holding zone for twenty boxes of Family Fun Day flyers, which were emptying rapidly. That day, Rachel and the lasses from the weekly prayer group had charged through the streets like papergirls on OTE commission, dredging up support from the depths of Bruton's backwaters, while Amy had given out two flyers – one to Suki (who was excited) and one to Selina (who shredded it).

Amy was currently reposing on the carpet, drawing on her arms with biro and looking like a miniature sailor from the seventeenth century. In front of her was an A4 sheet of paper, onto which she appeared to have poured a very small beach.

"Are you trying to make your own holiday?" Tom enquired, smiling down at his daughter and the tiny sand dune.

"No, Daddy – my holiday is upwards in Scotchland. With Grandad Smelly."

"Northwards, not upwards. Scotland, not Scotchland. And… yes, OK, I'll permit that last one."

"Yes, Daddy."

Amy's education had yet to help her grasp that north on a map was not the same as "upwards", but she proceeded to tell Tom that her class was doing a project about sand, and that every child had been given a small pouch of it to take home and examine under a magnifying glass.

Somewhere there's a beach volleyball team wondering why their knees are more grazed than usual.

"Mrs Hunter says that all the little tiny bits of little sand look the same until you see them under a mikeyscope."

"Who's Mikey Scope? Is he a boy in your class? Is he… is he your boyfriend?"

Amy leapt up and punched Tom on the knee with that embarrassed hilarity that can be guaranteed simply by mentioning the word "boyfriend" to a six-year-old girl.

"Silly Daddy! A mikeyscope makes you see things that are really small look reeeaaallly big."

"Maybe we could borrow it to look at our bank balance," Rachel quipped from across the room.

"We might need to upgrade to the Hubble telescope for that," Tom added, and his wife pouted affectionately.

Amy re-applied herself to the inky scribbles on her arms, and Rachel sought her husband's help in a private naming ceremony. Her weekly ladies' prayer group was growing exponentially – something of which Tom, whose professional angst was decreasing exponentially, now felt reassuringly proud – and to help with logistics, Rachel was looking for an umbrella term to facilitate its organisation.

"Jean suggested 'Woman on Woman', but I said I thought that might be misleading. Ironically, we'd probably have quite a few men turning up."

"Yes. Although if that's the way to attract chaps, maybe I should start a ministry called 'Woman on Woman'?"

"Nope."

The husband and wife combo thrashed it out for a while, hooking, reeling in and then releasing back into the waters names such as "The Bruton Bible Babes", "Desperate (for God) Housewives", and "Ladyplace".

In the end, after a gruelling brainstorming session, they decided on "The Women's Therapeutic Fellowship".

Yes, there's no way that could be misconstrued.

Chapter 15

Shoulder, Arms

Tom Hillingthwaite – or Big Fat Tom Hillingthwaite, as his wife was calling him affectionately – had started losing weight.

Since his move down from Nottinghamshire to Bruton, Tom had gained an excess two stones, which hung like millstones around his vital organs and meant that "Bunyan bladder" was no longer Tom's only burdensome quirk.

Rachel had said that she would love Tom no matter what his size, but she had also said that seeing him in swimming trunks brought to mind slaughtered poultry. Subsequently, she had put him on a Draconian diet of smoothies and juices.

"Hahaha, look at me!" Amy hooted, lumbering into the kitchen with Selina the cat under her Roundhouse Primary School cardigan.

"What are you doing with Selina?" Tom asked, between sips of lime and cauliflower smoothie.

"She's your belly – you're Big Fat Tom Hillingthwaite!"

"Amy, my love," Rachel interceded, "it's not appropriate for you to say that to your father. If you're going to call him anything, call him Big Fat Daddy. OK?"

Selina the renegade belly cat wriggled her way free and zipped out of sight, traumatised.

I wish my tummy would do that.

As Tom crossed the threshold of Roundhouse Primary once more that morning, a particularly limey mouthful of smoothie brought a spontaneous grimace to his slightly wonky facial features – a grimace that lingered long after his taste buds had recovered from the citrus assault.

From inside the head teacher's office, audible through the walls of plaster and juvenile stench, Tom could hear voices – two very recognisable voices – elevated in discord. It was Kathy and Petefeast.

A famous phrase, regularly spouted by Christians in the West, reads thus: "What would Jesus do?" The idea is that one considers how Jesus would approach any given situation, and then follows that same course of action. One of the reasons for Tom's recent downturn in social cataclysms was that he had been experimenting with a similar phrase: "What would Tom Hillingthwaite do?" The idea was that Tom would consider how he, himself, would approach any given situation, and then do totally the opposite. The results so far had been miraculous.

With Sherlockian assiduity, Tom deduced that in this situation his standard approach would almost certainly end with him bowing incongruously. This course of action wasn't necessary, and so Tom just waited in the lobby, listening.

"… not the time or the place…"

"… but I don't understand…"

"… huge mistake…"

"… king mean mistake…"

Tom couldn't distinguish all the fury-powered salvos from within the office, but he tapped enough intel to piece together a theme.

Suddenly, the door opened and Petefeast came fuming down the corridor in his rugby shirt and army shorts. Kathy stood boldly in her doorway, in tears.

"It's not over!" Petefeast shot back over his shoulder.

"It is, Pete. It is…"

When Petefeast clocked Tom loitering in the lobby, the former paratrooper's whole body stiffened. He looked upon Tom as a beefy flanker looks upon a midget scrum half who has tried to "run it" from a breakdown. Petefeast's pace quickened. Tom's ample belly would ensure he couldn't outrun the PE teacher – although the excess stomach padding might offer his kidneys some invaluable protection.

Fortuitously, the distance between the two men allowed time for Petefeast to recover enough professional dignity to stop himself from drop-kicking Tom. Instead, he came within biting distance and whispered, very gently and very cruelly, "Just you wait, little man… just you wait."

WWTHD? He would say something… OK, then, I won't say anything.

Pete removed himself from the two-man scrum and strode back to his classroom.

Tom looked down the corridor at Kathy. She smiled faintly at Tom, but raised her palm to hand off any conversations. Shaking her head, a tissue in her hand, she closed the door to her office and turned the key in the lock.

Well done, girl… Well done.

* * *

Tom and Jake spent their weekly session reading comics, and, to keep Mrs Quinn as happy as someone like her could ever hope to be, they filled in a couple of the patronising exercises from her special folder. Tom had actually found the "thinking chair" empty for once, and needed to knock on Mrs Quinn's door to retrieve Jake; for the first time ever, the young lad hadn't been pre-emptively ejected for agitating.

Before they reached their allocated cubby hole, Tom's plap-plapping plimsolls lost purchase with the newly mopped tiled floor and sent him crashing to the ground in a heap.

"I'm fine, I'm fine. It's OK, Jake, I'm fine."

"Why d'you keep falling over?" Jake asked, his eyebrows scrunched. It wasn't how Tom had imagined Jake's first full sentence to him would sound.

"Why do I keep falling, you say? Erm... so I can learn to pick myself up, I suppose."

Part way through a basic comprehension question on "Behaviour", Jake stopped writing and asked another question.

"Do you run that club?"

"What club's that, Jake?"

"Community centre."

"What, Burn? Well, I don't run it, but I do help out from time to time when they're short of staff."

"Can I come?"

Eh?

"Eh?"

"Live near there." Jake was fidgety, absent-mindedly using a pencil to tap out his heartbeat on the desk.

"Well, yes... of c... that's... yes – yes, of course you can come."

"OK."

"OK!"

Keep calm, Tom. Don't hula. Don't do any accents. Just hold it together.

Later, as Tom attempted to make his exit, Mrs Quinn's voice sucked him back down the corridor with "Ahem, excuse me, Mr Hillingthwaite?"

"Mrs Quinn?"

She looked suspicious – even more so than usual.

"What have you been doing with Jake – or should I say, *to* Jake?"

"Well, we've been doing the exercises that you asked us to do."

"Hmmm… Jake seems remarkably placid at the moment. I suspect you've been trying to indoctrinate him into your cult."

"Cult? You mean Christianity – the most widely held world-view on earth?"

I possibly shouldn't have said that.

"Truth isn't a popularity contest, Mr Hillingthwaite – which is probably favourable for someone like you." Her stitched-up wound of a smile was stretched to breaking point.

"Have you thought that maybe your special folder of exercises is just proving successful?" Tom asked with feigned earnestness.

"Don't patronise me. No, you're up to something – so be warned. Any religious guff that I catch wind of, and you'll be out of here… as will darling Kathy."

Unhelpful words were threatening to bubble out of Tom's mouth. He popped them just in time. Mrs Quinn saw the effort, and smiled again.

"Deal with it," she said in a perversely maternal way, coiling back to her classroom.

That's your new catchphrase, is it, milady?

Tom would kick the dust from his feet, allow her to hate him, and get on with the business of loving the people who needed it.

For once, Jesus and Tom Hillingthwaite would do the same thing.

* * *

It was somewhat fitting, given his wife's culinary embargo on anything with an actual taste, that Tom was taking up resident chaplaincy at one of the local gymnasiums: Fitnicity. It would give Tom a chance to minister to new (sweat-drenched) faces, while affording him the opportunity to shift some of his calorific midriff.

"Have fun, honeybunny," Rachel said between mouthfuls of Twix. "And leave the headband."

"But I thought it might…"

"Leave it."

As a gym, Fitnicity was going through something of a rebranding, and as he arrived Tom saw that the original signage, with the tagline "Gym'll fix it", was being taken down – wisely, in Tom's opinion. There was another sign going up with the tagline "Get fit or die trying".

No wonder they need a chaplain.

Tom entered the gym, and a third sign asked him to "Smell the Fitness". It was the same smell, Tom thought, as that of the abattoir in which he had worked for a week as a sixth-former.

Tom was met at the frosted-glass reception by Bradley, the immaculately haired Duty Manager, with street cred from the University of Life and a Sports Science Diploma from Keele. He offered Tom a coffee (which he declined) and a glass of water (which he accepted). Tom would also have accepted a nostril purge, but it wasn't offered.

Bradley presented Tom with a Fitnicity-branded polo shirt, and then led him through the guided tour, which mainly involved nodding obligingly at people in Lycra.

"I think you'll enjoy it here, Tom. It's not the cheapest gym in town, but it is the best. The guys here work hard and play hard, so I hope you do the same."

"I certainly like to work hard. I suppose I also like to play hard."

If by "play" you mean "sit down", and by "hard" you mean "often".

Bradley didn't mean that, so Tom just nodded appreciatively at a muscular man on a cross-trainer.

"I've had your official title printed on the back of the shirt, so just treat the place like *mi casa su casa*. We good?"

"Cool beans," Tom said, name-checking that night's dinner.

Before he could get to work chaplainising the fitness freaks, Tom had to have his membership card registered. Bradley swaggered down to reception, where the girl behind the desk was using the laminator to seal pictures of her boyfriend. Bradley sorted Tom's membership photo by flourishing a web cam in his direction without warning, startling him slightly, and a minute later Tom was presented with a membership card in the name of Tim Hollinghtwat, with a picture that made him look as though some nuclear testing had been carried out on his face.

It's the look I always go for on official photos.

Tom set to changing into his chaplain's outfit. Not feeling comfortable with his own body shape (he was still in "Large Sea Mammal Joins Gym Shocker" territory) he had no burning desire to enter the changing rooms. Plus, if the smell above ground was bad, he shuddered to think what subterranean odours might await him. So he returned to his car and hastily changed into his personalised polo shirt.

"Where's your moustache?" the girl at reception asked when he came back in.

"I've never had one," Tom replied.

He drew up a mental chaplainising plan (or cha-plan) and decided to make three gentle circuits of the gym area, just to dip his toe in the water. He would then take a brisk walk around the swimming pool, where he wouldn't dip his toe in the water. As cha-plans went, it was foolproof.

Tom believed that how he walked around the gymnasium was key to the members' acceptance of him. With so many creatined egos on show, it was important to strike the right balance between self-assurance and aloofness.

Initially, Tom struggled to get it right, experimenting with numerous different gaits, none of which quite worked. First of all he tried a patrol, but that made him feel like a sadistic head teacher, punishing naughty children with overly physical detentions. Next he shifted to a sort of promenade, Victorian gent-style, but one really needs to be arm-in-arm for that, and Tom didn't think Bradley looked that tactile. Parading didn't work either: it made him look as if he was showing off – and of all the peacocks in the gym, Tom had by far the least attractive plumage.

Ultimately, he settled for a kind of saunter, which made him look a bit furtive and mentally peripheral, but it was the best he could do.

On the third lap of the exercise floor, by which time he was building up quite a collection of sweat patches, Tom spotted Petefeast, who was sprinting along barbarically on one of the treadmills. When the sights of the former soldier fell on the former rug-seller, a look of hateful glee was loaded into the chamber of his eyes. With military precision, he hopped off the treadmill and started crossing the training mats towards Tom, wrapping his sweat towel round his fist as he neared. Tom wanted to get away, but all the modes of transport that he might have chosen for his escape – bicycle, rowing boat, cross-country skis – were all attached to the floor and thus useless.

With no professional dignity needed here, Petefeast could bench-press Tom to his heart's content...

"Oi, Tom!"

Tom and Petefeast both looked towards the voice, and Tom's face lifted. It was Dazza, pumping iron in the weights section, shirtless in posturing virility. He laid down his dumbbells and sauntered over towards Tom. Petefeast circled round and headed towards the showers, his fist-towel unfurling.

With relief and friendliness merging into giddiness, Tom greeted Dazza like a brother – a brother he hadn't seen for years and whom he had heard, through official Reuters networks, had perished.

"Hi, Dazza – you've no idea how nice it is to see you."

"All right, geezer?" There was definite inflection in the voice as Dazza said "All right". He was genuinely asking if Tom was all right.

"Yes, I'm fine – now, anyway. Are you having it large?"

"Ha, ha. Could say that, yeah. What are you doing here, anyways? Didn't realise you were into this sort of thing."

"Oh yes, I'm pretty into my gym… nastics – yes, for sure. I don't pump some irons very often but… yes."

"Cool. It's good you're here actually. My training partner hasn't turned up. Can you spot me?"

It seemed an odd request on Dazza's part.

"Certainly, sir… there you are."

Surely a more pertinent venture would be trying to spot his training partner.

Dazza peered at Tom's guileless smile through narrowed eyes. "Mate, are you for real?"

"Sorry?"

"Don't think I've ever met anyone who knows less about sport. What you actually doing here?"

"Oh, I'm the chaplain." Tom turned round so Dazza could see the back of his polo shirt.

"Oh, ha, ha, right! Where's your funny walk?"

"Well, yes, as you've noticed I've been struggling to find a suitable gait."

"Er… right. What's the point of it, though?"

Tom explained what a chaplain did, and why he did it, and

then he helped Dazza finish off some weight-training, during which time Tom found it a piece of cake to "spot" him.

As Dazza hefted the iron up and down, he explained to Tom which muscles were doing what when he was doing what he was doing. His voice was so deep and vibrant, listening to him was like having one's ears syringed.

When Dazza asked if Tom wanted to have a go himself, the chaplain was slightly taken aback – he had been lying when he said he liked pumping some irons – but looking weak in Dazza's presence was not a health-conscious plan.

He's an alpha male, whereas I'm not. I'm not even beta or delta. I'm more epsilon. Still, I'm definitely a male, as my unfeasibly tight shorts prove.

So Tom lay back on the padded water-board, hastily composing his own 1980s montage music in his mind, and got ready to feel the burn.

"Do you know what you rep?" asked Dazza.

This was another one of those phrases that proper men used which sounded as though it could mean a number of things, but would almost certainly turn out not to mean whatever Tom initially thought it meant. So he caught the words "I rep for Jesus" just before they spilled out of his mouth and said, "No."

Dazza looked him up and down and decided that they should start him at Level 7. It was a bit too heavy... as were 6 and 5 and 4, but Tom could confidently lift Level 3, and managed ten weight-liftings before his torso was consumed with an unquenchable fire.

"Ha! Well done, geezer, you did it!"

Dazza helped Tom up from the floor where he had crumpled and was dry-heaving.

"Thanks. That was a new and fun experience for me," Tom was completely unable to say. It came out as "Hoargghhh..."

"Mate, thanks for them cakes by the way. They was nice, cheers."

"Oh, it was my pleasure. We had a surplus and so we just distributed them to people we knew," Tom would have needed much better stamina in order to say. It came out as "Hoargghhh..."

"Anyway, gotta go, geezer – don't have a washing machine so I need to get to the laundrette before it closes."

"Hoargghhh... wait... I can do your washing."

"Nah mate, s'all good – just down the road."

Tom waggled a finger in admonition while he breathlessly regained his speaking voice.

"Please, Dazza, let me do your washing for you. We've got a nice washing machine, and it's no trouble."

"What, really? Oh right... well, yeah, that'd be great if it's all right?"

"Of course it is. Meet me outside the changing rooms in ten minutes – I'll have stopped retching by then, I hope."

As Tom made his way back to the car, Dazza's sweaty clothes in a carrier bag under his arm, his body creaking and straining like an ancient galleon in a storm, a man walking behind him down the steps joked, "Where's your stick?"

"Well, I need one at this rate."

It wasn't until Tom got home later and stripped off his polo shirt that he finally understood what all the obscure questions had referred to: Where's your moustache... funny walk... stick?

In bold letters on the back of his polo shirt was printed the word "Chaplin".

Chapter 16

He Stands at the Door and Knocks

Tom Hillingthwaite was happy. Happy. He was enjoying his job and feeling settled where he lived; his desert places were blooming into a beautiful Eden.

The memory of the comedy night fiasco – after which he had passed sobbing through a long dark night of the soul – was still there, and twice since then Tom had bolted awake in the night shouting, "Where are you, Father?"

But the guilt and the shame were losing their battle for Tom's spirit, and his worth was no longer rooted in his abilities as a Community Builder, which – much to everyone's surprise, not least his own – were dramatically improving anyway.

I think I've finally crossed the Jordan.

Tom had even engaged in his first-ever conversation with the Kung-Fu Gardener. Their paths had crossed on bin collection day, and Tom had thought he seemed nice in a "you wouldn't want to smell his bedroom" sort of way. During their brief conversation, Tom had explained part of his role as Community Builder, and the man in the karate suit divulged that his brother

196

(a former soldier) worked at Roundhouse Primary, but that they never saw each other. The Kung-Fu Gardener had then suggested that he and Tom act out a Tae-Kwon-Do-based role-play where the KFG would play himself and Tom would play a wheelie bin. Tom politely declined and went to stand round the corner (without a vase of Vimto this time) until the KFG re-entered his house.

Even better news was that Jake had followed up on his question about the youth group, and had turned up at Burn the very next week (although the group was now called CrossWords, after a near-fatal mix up with the fire brigade and a narrowly avoided lawsuit).

Jake had scuff-scraped in, read some comics, played on the PlayStation with Hezza, and scuff-scraped out with a smile on his face and a "Bye" from his lips.

Most of all, though, Tom was exhilarated by the gently growing bump in Rachel's belly. A new life was coming into the world, and into a world where his/her father was feeling modicumly in control.

It would soon be time for the twelve-week scan, and Tom and Rachel were sleeping on different wards when it came to their prognoses on the matter. For Rachel, the scan would be a chance to catch that first moving glimpse of the baby, all fearfully and wonderfully made, whereas for Tom it would provide a singular opportunity to look bemused at what might as well be a close-up picture of the moon.

At Amy's twelve-week scan, Rachel had asked for several print-outs of the sonogram, and made haste to show the picture to all her female friends, who gathered round and said things like, "Ooh, isn't it sweet," and "Look, you can see the head," and "Have you got a name for it yet?" Tom found this odd because, to his mind, the elephant in the room was that you couldn't actually see anything. Unusually for Tom, however, he hadn't made the mistake of using the idiom "elephant in the room" with his pregnant wife; after all, months of Tunnock's tea cake addiction had meant that Tom himself was still the elephant in most rooms.

But life was good. It was really good. It was BYOB.

Birth Your Own Baby.

The main thing was that the Hillingthwaites were doing things together, as a team. The lone wolf had finally come back to the bosom of the pack.

Despite the joy and gladness to be found in and around Hillingthwaite Manor, there was still important work to be done. The Family Fun Day was approaching apace, and the flyering needed to fly up a notch. All the equipment for the event – ice-cream vans, dunk tank, politically incorrect Sumo suits – had been confirmed, and now it was simply about the attendees actually attending.

It was the second time that Tom had been out door-knocking, but there had been a few problems with his first foray: specifically that knocking on an old lady's door, claiming to be from the church but having no way of proving it (his only ID being a gym membership card on which a man named Hollinghtwat looked petrified) hadn't got Tom any business, but had got him questioned by police.

"If you're going to visit on behalf of the church, you need to look like it," he told Rachel, sharing his quandary. "I just don't have any recognisable church attire."

A look of creepy amusement tip-toed its way onto Rachel's face.

"You say that, Tom…"

She made a couple of phone calls, and three hours later Tom left the house suited and booted, looking much more apt for door-to-door visits. And people probably wouldn't notice that he was dressed in the seamless cassock of a sexy fetish vicar

– after all, it was pretty much the same costume as a normal vicar, but held together by prayer and Velcro rather than good old-fashioned embroidery.

* * *

Tom couldn't get round to every house in Bruton, so he was paying Hezza and his gangster mate Jozee (who had just received a conditional offer from Warwick University) to drop some flyers through letter boxes on the other side of town. They wouldn't do this. Tom knew that they wouldn't do this. They knew that he knew, and he knew that they knew that he knew that they wouldn't do this. Everybody knew.

Still, the sun was out and Tom was quite enjoying the unpressurised flyer drop in his refreshingly airy outfit.

It's amazing how friendly people can be when you don't try to convert them instantly to Christianity.

The range of welcomes Tom received from people was wide and staggering. One woman on Rosemary Lane mistook his knock on the door for the weekly supermarket delivery she was expecting, and when Tom insisted that he didn't have any groceries for her, she told him he had just talked himself out of a customer. Another open door revealed a house of student males, who asked if Tom would like to make up a round-robin tournament of a game called Pro Evolution Soccer. Tom told them he was more Pro Creation and, to show him how funny they found that, the door closed abruptly in his face.

He found one house where the man who answered turned out to be a woman, but the sort of woman who might have featured as the main protagonist in an Elizabethan sea shanty. Still, plenty of flyer-recipients admitted interest in the Fun Day and, rather like a wanted criminal ringing a police station, Tom curtailed conversations before any of his character flaws could be traced. It was another small success.

From behind one of the knocked doors, a wiry woman squinted at Tom from an attractive but worry-drenched face that he initially struggled to place. The woman registered surprise that Tom wasn't her friendly neighbourhood drug-dealer, but when he showed her the flyer she invited him in for a "cuppa".

Tom was led into the kitchen through a fuggy haze of what even he knew to be marijuana smoke. The young woman flicked on the kettle, which was standing next to a foil package of what probably weren't tasty sandwiches.

Where do I know her from?

"So, tell me all about this malarkey then, Reverend."

Tom cagily explained what the Family Fun Day would involve, wondering whether she was actually the sort of clientele he was trying to attract, and whether he should call the police about the sordid drugs lab he had just uncovered.

I could be a hero and make a citizen's arrest.

He concluded that if the police turned up and found the man recently questioned for door-knocking was now wearing a rogue vicar's outfit, he might find himself on the front page of the *Bruton Gazette* – and not for his Billy-Graham-like outreach ability.

The young woman listened to Tom's Fun Day pitch as she rolled herself a joint, then sploshed down a cup of tea in front of him. Tom had reverted to his previously held beverage puritanism and so caffeine was back off the agenda, but he doubted the house held any fruit tea – and he didn't want to research what varieties of leaf there were, in case he accidentally joined a drug ring.

"Could I have two sugars with that, please?" he asked instead.

"Two sugars? It's ever so bad for ya, ya know!" The young woman took a long drag on her homemade cigarette.

Tom was feeling morally violated, his jovial banter burning to a stub. He wanted to traffick himself out of there as quickly as possible, so he took a sip of tea, grimaced, placed it by the sink and made his excuses.

"Lots more people to get round, so goodbye for now."

"No, you must come and see my old man first."

"Who? Where?"

"In the living room – come through, vicar."

Reluctantly, Tom followed her out of the kitchen and into the living room, not unafraid that he might collapse from the fumes and wake up in the deserts of New Mexico. He was feeling sick – and strangely hungry.

I could do with a tasty sandwich, but I'll get one from Londis.

"Living room" was an overly grandiose term for something as bleak as the space Tom entered. "Existing room" would have been more suitable – the only decoration being a minuscule jungle of illegal foliage surrounding the TV. It had the look of the Sub-Tropical Swimming Paradise at Center Parcs, Tom thought.

Although there's no world-class wave pool, and at Center Parcs you're not allowed to smoke the scenery.

Tom saw no sign of the woman's "old man", though.

"Is he playing hide and seek?" Tom asked, his mind flashing back to the day he had stumbled upon Kathy and Petefeast's indiscretion.

I need to stop assuming grown adults are playing hide and seek – they almost never are.

"No, he's here, look…" The young woman picked up a framed photo from on top of the TV. The frame was the only thing in the room that had been given any attention in the cleaning stakes. The photo within was of a man in his late twenties – not really an "old man" at all – sitting on a sand dune with a towel around his shoulders. He was smiling at the camera, head tilted, with one eyebrow raised and his tongue out. One wouldn't have called him handsome.

"Would ya look at that face?" she said. "He's such a joker."

"Is he at work?"

"Nah, I dunno where he is."

The worry which drenched this young woman's face had drip-dripped over time and soaked her through. Her expression reached Tom through the sweet-smelling smoke like the sight of a Ripper victim in London Town. And he knew her.

She was the woman who had given him directions to the Baptist church all those months ago. The woman who had asked him to pray for her son whose dad had just left.

Vicky? The name sprung to mind and, thinking it to be a word of knowledge, Tom spoke it out.

"Vicky?"

"Yeah. How did you know that?"

Yes.

"We've met before. You were sitting on a bollard on the High Street. I prayed for your boy – do you remember?"

Suddenly Vicky was looking at Tom, and remembering. Her eyes were all lit up with warmth. Tom bound his own cynicism – the cynicism that had almost caused him to walk out – and loosed a big smile in her direction.

"How is your boy?"

"Oh, well, ya know what, he's OK, yeah. Better than me. Oh, and thank you."

Even through her agonies, her eyes were now all lit up with warmth for Tom.

"You're welcome, Vicky. I'm glad to hear that about your boy."

The front door had been left open when Vicky invited Tom in, and now a third person had entered the house. Hearing a man's voice from the living room, the newcomer pushed through the door with a hopeful cry of, "Dad?"

When he saw that it wasn't his dad, the look of sadness on the boy's face nearly broke Tom's heart.

Oh, my goodness. How…?

Tom needed no spiritual prompts to know this name.

"Hi, Jake."

On Jake's face, sadness turned to confusion turned to hope. "Hi."

Tom paused a moment to breathe in his options. Then he turned to Vicky and said, "Shall we have another cup of tea?"

When the kettle had boiled and Jake had recovered, Tom sat with Vicky and her son in their leafy lounge, and gushed with pride about how Jake had progressed and how well he was doing in their sessions.

Vicky puffed out smoke and gratitude in equal measure, while Jake sat looking shy but not unhappy. He even offered Tom a Jaffa Cake, which Tom gratefully accepted.

Even drug lairs provide better refreshments than churches.

Then an idea eureka-ed itself to Tom.

"Hey, Vicky. Me and the other leaders at CrossWords are taking some of the young people on a paintballing trip this weekend. I wonder if you'd allow me to pay for Jake to go? We could pick him up in the minibus, sort him out with lunch and so on… Hezza will be there, Jake."

"Whad'ya think, son?"

Jake nodded.

"Yeah, I wanna go. He's fun."

"A-ha, yes! Hezza is indeed quite the card," Tom agreed.

"No, not him. You."

Oh…

"Oh…"

Tom finished his horrendous cup of tea, set a pick-up time for Saturday's excursion, and went to leave.

"See ya soon, Tom," Jake said, waving a Jaffa Cake.

"See ya soon, Jake," Tom mimicked. "See you soon, Vicky. I'll just leave the Fun Day flyer here then, shall I?"

"Yeah, thanks. In fact, leave me a few, will ya? I'm running low on Rizlas."

Tom left Jake's house chastising his own piety, but rejoicing that, in spite of himself, the situation had been fixed.

On the one hand, he was an idiot. He had pre-judged Vicky because of the clichés he had applied to her, and felt suitably ashamed that his puritanism wasn't just confined to beverages. He had so peremptorily dismissed a young woman battling with drugs, only to find that she wasn't just some fiend – but the mother of his friend. She had definitely made bad choices, but Tom had been too quick to write her off as a stereotype.

Every grain of sand looks the same until you see it under the mikeyscope.

On the other hand, it seemed as though there were forces at work beyond Tom's moralism. It had been a great visit: Jake thought that Tom was funny, and he was opening up more each time Tom saw him. The lad was making huge progress, and the high which that gave Tom was more effective than any drug.

"And if you hadn't worn that stripping vicar's outfit," Rachel pointed out, "you wouldn't have ventured out at all."

"Yes, I suppose that's true," Tom chuckled.

"So maybe you've been altogether too judgmental about too many people?"

Then, to show what he thought about his wife's most recent question, Tom removed the sexy fetish vicar costume, placed it back in its bag, and spent an hour in the shower, flaying himself with a pumice stone.

Chapter 17

Saved by the Dumb-bell

Tom was tucking into a delicious meal of chicken kiev with chips and an extra chicken kiev (it was the extra chicken kiev that turned it from a good meal into a great one), when a muted *dunna dunna dunna dunna* beeped from his jacket pocket.

O.M.Giddy Aunt. Might as well get it over with…

"Hello, Harvey."

"Ah, hello, Thomas – nice to hear your voice for a change."

It was Tom's primary overseer from Jesus4All (formerly the Turn or Burn Gospel Coalition) once again disturbing family time with his communication.

For the past couple of months, Tom had tried to avoid direct contact with Harvey whenever possible, owing to a totally unblemished salvation scoreboard at Tom's end. But the man was still his boss – as unsupportive as Tom found him – and so, consequently, Tom had been answering Harvey's calls roughly once a fortnight.

"We're just in the middle of tea at the moment, Harvey," Tom said through a mouthful of hot garlic butter. "Can I call you back later?"

"Well, you see, Thomas, this is symptomatic of the problem, isn't it? Your job doesn't seem to be a priority."

"Sorry? That's not true – I'm just eating at the moment."

"Yes, you've been eating quite a bit from what I hear. Anyway, listen, we're not happy. You've been in Brighton… is it Brighton? Bruton… you've been in Bruton goodness knows how long now, and you've failed to win a single soul."

"Yes, but…"

"No, no, no, Thomas, your excuses have to stop. All this bluster about building community is just a veil for your incompetence…" Harvey cleared his throat with the rattling death-throes of a cough.

"Please consider this a verbal warning, Thomas. Your written warning is in the post. One more, and you're out."

Verbal warning? Written warning?

Tom watched a pea roll off Amy's plate onto the floor. Where his daughter had been like a pig in muck since their move to Bruton, Tom had been in a pigging muck a lot of the time. But not any more. Now he loved his job! And he had hoped that the good work he was doing in building relationships would be viewed as a bridge for a more long-term outreach strategy. Harvey and the other two Jesus4All benefactors, though, didn't agree; they wanted cut-and-dried results.

"Are you still there, Thomas?"

"Yes."

"Yes, well, we're travelling down to see you for this Family Fun Day next week. I do hope that there will at least be some sort of formal Gospel presentation."

There wasn't going to be a formal Gospel presentation.

It's a Family Fun Day. No family has ever had fun at a formal Gospel presentation.

"I…the plan was just to…"

"The plan, Thomas – God's plan, and therefore your plan

– is to bring people to faith and repentance. Great hopes we had for you, my lad, great hopes. Our man in Mercia has been baptising people in the river in their droves. He's a veritable John the Baptist. Which biblical character would you say you are, Thomas? Think on, and we shall see you shortly. Every good wish!"

Tom didn't know which biblical character he was. He did know that, unless things changed quickly, he would be out of a Job. He stabbed a piece of bread-crumbed chicken with his fork and studied the skewered meat closely. Then, looking ruefully through his kitchen window onto the cul-de-sac of Dews Close, Tom saw, standing centrally on the road, an old man with a broken nose and salt-and-pepper beard.

Of course he's there. He only turns up when things are looking grim.

Tom nodded imperceptibly at the man, then matter-of-factly returned to his food. When he looked up again a few moments later, the man had gone.

See you next time, then.

Tom had no idea how to hold in tension his boss's orders and what he knew to be true: that here, now, in Bruton, serving people with the love of God was more effective than flaying them with the fear of God.

His chances of surviving Harvey's visit appeared about as slim as the chances of his chicken kiev fun-running back to the farm.

But then the miracle came.

* * *

Tom was back at Fitnicity, the gym where you got fit or died trying. Tom wasn't yet fit, but he wasn't yet dead, and Rachel's enforced smoothie diet was working wonders. While his ideal weight was still some way out to sea, at least he no longer looked like a whale that had been washed ashore and integrated into society.

Tom's cha-plan was coming along nicely, too. He was getting to know some familiar faces at the gym and drumming up support for the Family Fun Day. One group of weightlifters – with veins so pronounced, their skin looked like a 3D map of European rivers – had even agreed to put on a show as part of the event (on completion of an impromptu Charlie Chaplin walk from Tom, which they filmed but promised never to upload but then put straight onto YouTube anyway). Tom didn't argue; one of his rules in life was never to argue with anyone whose pulse is visible in their forehead.

Tom was fetching a complimentary glass of water for a lady on an elliptical trainer when he heard the familiar voice of Dazza beckoning him to one side. Tom sauntered over (he was by now convinced that sauntering was by far the most suitable walk for a gym) and saw the grin on Dazza's face getting bigger and wider as he approached, like a joyous horizon.

"Hi Dazza, what's going–"

"Tom, mate, I've become a Christian!"

"No, you haven't," denied the professional evangelist.

"I 'ave, mate. I've met him – I've met Jesus. It's ******* brilliant!"

"Come again?" Tom couldn't quite believe his ears. "But we've never talked about Jesus."

"No, I know, but Simon doesn't 'ave to say it, mate! I didn't even know you was one of 'em until I saw you with that tee shirt. But then I was bored at home – I don't live with no one, see – and I started watching all them God channels on telly... and it got me." Dazza shrugged. "I dunno how to explain it – I jus' thought, 'Yeah, that makes sense.'"

Tom Hillingthwaite had been trained to evangelise. He had never been taught what to do after that. He stood there, an epsilon male looking into the bouncing, giddy face of an alpha gorilla. And he started to cry. He cried with joy and relief and wonder and confusion and then Dazza hugged him and patted him on the back and it really hurt but he didn't care.

"Let's 'ave it!" Tom sobbed into Dazza's shoulder.

"It's finetastic, mate, is what it is. ******* finetastic!"

Minutes later, Tom and Dazza were sitting in Tom's car, grappling with this most unlikely of conversions. The woman on the elliptical trainer had been left waterless and was starting to dehydrate.

"But what do I do now, though, geezer?" Dazza was keen to pursue this, but baffled as to how.

Tom bit his lip as he thought about it. Across a misty lake of confusion, Harvey's rasping criticism rowed into view.

Coming to the Family Fun Day… man from Mercia baptising people in the river… no more excuses, Thomas…

"I've got it! Let's baptise you – at the Family Fun Day."

Dazza looked no less baffled.

"What does that mean? Like a baby?"

"Infant baptism isn't biblical."

"Eh?"

"Sorry, I'm excited – we can come back to that bit. Look, I'll walk you through it all – it's something people did in the Bible to show that they were being washed spiritually clean. There's going to be a dunk tank at the Fun Day. It's more for punishing witches traditionally, but we could use it – after the crowds leave, just with people you want to invite. What do you think?"

"Yeah, OK… yeah, let's 'ave it."

~~Tom~~ God had done it. The salvation had come, and now when the bosses from Jesus4All (formerly the Turn or Burn Gospel Coalition) turned up to the Family Fun Day, they would see with their own eyes the fruits of Tom's labour.

BYOB – Baptise Your Own Buddy. I like it.

* * *

As respite from the Family Fun Day preparation, Tom was going paintballing. Rachel suggested that this would be the most manly thing he had ever done since he ran over a pheasant on their honeymoon.

"The death of that pheasant was almost entirely accidental," Tom insisted. "And besides, animals are animals, but I could never kill another man."

"You're not being asked to kill another man," Rachel said. "It's paintball – the most you're going to do is decorate them."

"Well, I don't like decorating either."

In truth, the idea of paintballing was terrifying to Tom.

It's like one of those laddish 18–30 holidays where thirty go and only eighteen come back.

When the leaders of the CrossWords youth group had met up to talk about the best places for a daytrip, Tom initially suggested Thorpe Towers. It was ultimately agreed that Thorpe Towers wouldn't be the destination for the excursion, because it didn't actually exist.

The other organisers then suggested that paintball would be a good way for the young lads to get some of their aggression out. Tom had counter-suggested that, alternatively, it might take a group of lads who already hunted in packs and teach them skills in weapons and tactics. Tom voted against paintballing, but lost the vote 4–1. He lost the subsequent recount by the same margin, and was told that he hadn't actually been invited to the meeting anyway.

The minibus that shuttled them out into the Wessex countryside looked, Tom thought, like the sort of vehicle they show on *Children in Need* just before asking viewers to "Give whatever you can". It was a contraption upon which Fred Flintstone would look and scoff.

On the ride over to Paintball Jungle (tagline: "Not for the paint-hearted") Tom tried to engage the young lads in so-called "banter". In Tom's mind, banter was the art of creating witty, spontaneous vignettes out of nothing, whereas for Hezza and co., it seemed to centre almost exclusively on calling one other gay. Tom wasn't prepared to stoop that low, but his attempts at witty spontaneous vignettes were also appalling.

However you define banter, I'm not very good at it.

Instead, Tom tried to doze, but was woken by Jozee writing the word "homo" on his cheek in biro.

The first casualty of war is political correctness.

* * *

The compound of Paintball Jungle was a large acreage of woodland leased from a local farmer by a couple of ex-squaddies, following their dishonourable discharge from the Wessex Fusiliers. From the moment of the minibus's juddering arrival, the former army men treated the group with a stern militarism, and Tom couldn't work out whether this was method acting to lace the day with realism, or simply a blatant refusal to accept that they weren't soldiers any more.

The group donned overalls and goggles, and un-racked the paintball guns from the armoury (which was a tent from Millets with the word "Armoury" spelled out in duct-tape).

While Tom was mentally putting on the helmet of salvation and breastplate of righteousness, Jake was having trouble finding overalls that didn't swamp him – most of them made him look like a tent peg trapped beneath a groundsheet. Tom rummaged around in a locker, and after some rolling up of sleeves and trouser legs, Jake was battle-ready.

"How do you feel?" Tom asked.

"Excited," Jake said, almost looking it. "Did you feel excited on your first time?"

"First time? Do you think I could stand this butcher's yard more than once?"

"Chill out, Tom," said Hezza, toting his gun in that brap-brapping way that has become so popular among middle-class teenagers. "It's gonna be sweeeeeet. Stick with me, Jakey-boy – I'm proper gangsta!"

Hezza wasn't gangsta. Living in the most affluent area of Bruton in a five-bedroom house with a conservatory and bespoke treehouse, he hadn't even met a gangsta. His private education had also been effective enough to teach him how to correctly spell the word "gangster".

The name of the day's game was "Ambush", and the aim was that Tom's team, Bravo Two Zero, would head out into the barren wilderness and lie in wait for the other team, Zero Dark Thirty, to patrol past them. If ZDT spotted them first and opened fire, Tom's team would lose. If, however, BTZ remained unspotted, they would then win the challenge by spraying the enemy with the full range of the Dulux Colour Chart in the form of small, painful pellets.

"It's a bit like hide and seek," one of the organisers joked, "but with a higher risk of permanent blindness." Nobody laughed.

Tom, deciding to engage with the day while daydreaming about setting up a place called Thorpe Towers, asked the disgraced former sergeant whether he could borrow some make-up. The sergeant said that yes, he could, so long as he called it camouflage and not make-up. Tom reluctantly agreed, and didn't mention the word "pedantic" in case the camouflage stick was handed to him via his lower intestine.

Tom took point and led his team out into the undergrowth to set up ambush. The number of bugs on the ground filled Tom with a sense of mortal dread, but he wanted to show strong leadership in front of Jake – and he doubted that any real soldier had ever surrendered due to creepy-crawlies. The members of Bravo Two Zero lay in silence, their bodies getting colder and damper, Tom reprimanding Hezza at one point for trying to smoke bracken.

The chill was prickly, and yet the soft grass, natural soundtrack and Tom's general lack of sleep conspired to send him into a deep nap. When he was woken abruptly – by Jozee trying to pick his pocket – Tom had totally lost his bearings and worried momentarily that he'd somehow been kidnapped.

"What's happening? Please… please, why me?"

"Sshhhh!" hissed his team in military unison.

After forty minutes, Tom and his paintballing acolytes were about to give up hope of winning the game and retreat back to HQ (which was another Millets tent) when suddenly they heard the footsteps of Zero Dark Thirty shuffling through the woods. As one, all the members of Bravo Two Zero tensed with expectation.

Had they been spotted? Had the smoke from Hezza's fern cigarette led the enemy in their direction? Were they moments away from being painted top-to-toe in defeat? The guns remained silent. They hadn't been spotted. And now the trap was set.

Tom felt adrenaline rattling through him in a way he had not experienced since that pheasant stepped out in front of his oncoming car. He felt amazing – strong and powerful and invincible and… like a real man. His troops were waiting obediently for his command to unleash hell.

He waited for the enemy to tread within whites-of-their-eyes territory, and was about to give the order to fire when he unleashed a fart of monstrous proportions. It came out of nowhere, as he had hoped the ambush would, and fairly rent the air in twain (in his peripheral vision he had a vague sense that a squirrel had fainted).

However, the titanic trump wasn't what gave them away. What gave them away was Tom's apology. His loud whisper of "Oh, I am sorry" laid a very obvious trail of breadcrumbs for the opposition, who opened fire into the bushes, splattering BTZ with globules of matt vinyl. Hezza, who lay directly behind Tom, tried to return fire but was immobilised by the fact that he had one sleeve over his nose and was retching.

Moments later, Tom and his comrades trudged out of the bushes, covered in non-lethal paint wounds. Tom felt silly and embarrassed, but the blow was softened by the fact that one of his platoon, disregarding the painful pummelling he had just received, was rolling in shrubbery, breathlessly giggling.

After months of disciplined contact, it had taken something as simple as escaped gas to make Jake laugh out loud.

At the close of play, back at the tents, Tom was paraded in front of the other gamers and given a special medal for "Worst Player". The former army sergeant declared that it was being awarded for "ill-timed use of chemical warfare".

On the way back in the minibus nobody wanted to sit by Tom, but Hezza did describe his windy outburst as "top banter", so there was that. Tom sat alone at the front, mildly wounded by embarrassment. Jake sat at the back of the bus, wincingly clutching his stomach – not from gunshot wounds, but from gut-wrenching laughter.

I shall claim a moral victory for that, I think.

Chapter 18

The "Fun" in Fundamental

The sun rose over Bruton Town in the same way it always did. But to Tom Hillingthwaite, sitting with a carrot and ginger smoothie in his kitchen, the remote ball of indomitable flame possessed an added glow that morning. The weatherman on the BBC had predicted heavy rain throughout the day for most of the South, but the sun had obviously upgraded to Sky and no longer watched terrestrial television.

Tom felt a warm front of emotion brush over him.

The whole Hillingthwaite family – except for Selina the cat, who remained stoically ambivalent about the Family Fun Day – were up with the dawn, readying themselves to head down to the Alvin Stardust Community Park. The festivities weren't due to commence until 10:30 a.m., but Tom arrived at 8.15 a.m. to help set up.

The good people at Baguette Behind Me Satan had sent over an early-morning batch of oven-fresh treats, and Tom circulated the different stalls and craft tables, chatting and handing out pastries.

"You must try a Danish," Tom told a blonde lady who was laying out teddy-bear soaps. Checking that Rachel wasn't looking,

215

he bit into the warm, forbidden Danish. It was like a party in his mouth where everyone was invited but they turned the music down after 10 p.m. and the guests left at a reasonable hour having first helped with the clear-up. It was Tom's ideal party.

The centrepiece of the event was the vast dunk tank in which, later on, Dazza would be baptismally plunged.

"You ever had anyone drown in one of these?" Tom asked the dunk tank overseer, a svelte Cornishman with the latest in beard fashion.

"Depends what you mean by drown," he replied, biting into a Belgian bun.

Tom decided to up his prayer output for the day.

Please, Lord, no drownings. Not today… And no other deaths, either, thanks. Please don't see this prayer as an exclusive request for the avoidance of one type of demise. I want that none should perish at this Family Fun Day. Amen.

The big question for the day, of course – after, "Would anybody die?" – was, "Would any families turn up and have fun?" Tom had managed to avoid any major outlay in hiring the sideshows (the council, moved and, frankly, confused that anything so altruistic was taking place, had underwritten the cost of the park and stalls) but that would all prove pyrrhic in its victory if nobody showed up. The flyering had been done and people had gushed their enthusiasm, but Tom was canny enough to realise that some people will do anything to get you off their doorstep.

He put aside six extra pastries as an emergency binge fund, hiding them in a bag behind the coconut shy.

But the sunshine held, and just after 10.30 a.m. people started to trickle down in human tributaries. A trickle became a stream became a torrent, and by midday the park was full of happy Brutonians, gallivanting on bouncy castles, smashing into one another in oversized Sumo suits, and consuming heart-attacks disguised as sweets.

Wayne the Tattooligan was there, and Catrina and Not-Carl and Anne and Kathy. They all greeted Tom in their own special way – some by embracing him fondly, some by locking themselves in a portaloo until he was out of sight. Even the Kung-Fu Gardener was there, standing on a duelling pedestal, shouting for challengers to meet him in pugil-stick combat.

Martin Hartnett was one of the later arrivals from Tom's inner circle (of which Martin constituted 180 degrees), promenading arm-in-arm with the perfumed lady from No. 1 Dews Close. Her self-fragrancing tendencies were under much better control now that she was courting Martin. Tom practically force-fed his friend a *pain au chocolat*.

"Tom, this all looks great!" Martin said.

"Thank you, kind sir."

"And thank you so much for getting those sewers fixed," the lady from No. 1 followed up. "If only everyone at the council was as diligent as you."

She had never quite grasped that Tom had nothing to do with civic office, but it was madness to keep explaining the same thing expecting a different result, so Tom said, "Thank you. I'll pass that news on to the mayor."

"No need – I think he's here somewhere… yes, he's by the burger van. I shall return…"

The lady from No. 1 tottered off on her Gucci platforms to talk to someone who actually did work with the council.

She'll probably ask him what he plans to do about the split over women bishops.

Martin smiled after his girlfriend with fondness. "Lovely lady, Tom!"

"She is indeed, Martin. Always liked her perfume."

"Oh, well, to be honest, Tom, I hadn't noticed. I lost my sense of smell in a chemistry lab in 1989."

"I'm sorry to hear that."

"Not to worry. Oddly, my sense of hearing has been heightened ever since."

"Oh, really, has it?"

"Pardon?"

"Aha! A good joke, Martin, if ever I heard one. Another *pain au chocolat*?"

The range of ages at the Family Fun Day was diverse, and for each age group there was something exciting to do. At one end of the park, Suki and Amy were hurling themselves down slides while, at the other, the Beetle Drivers of the Round Table were doing the only thing they ever wanted to do aside from sleep.

"I thought there was going to be a petting zoo?" Beetle Drive Merlin said to Tom, as the host brought them a complimentary tray of polystyrene cups brimming with tea.

"Ah, yes. Bit of a change of plan there."

There had been plans for a local farmer to bring a donkey and a pig for the children to pet, but the donkey had apparently fallen off a bridge, and a single pig didn't constitute a petting zoo. The farmer had still brought the pig, but was calling it a hog roast.

In a last-minute bid to save the petting-zoo attraction, Catrina had brought along her new rabbit, Mitsy II (she had never found original Mitsy, but hoped it had found a good home), while Wayne the Tattooligan had brought Boobies the dog, who was tethered to a post and running madly round in circles.

All the lads from CrossWords had rolled up en masse on their bikes – a cheeky counterbalance to the two mounted police patrolling the perimeter. Hezza and Jozee were present, and were racing round the park's circuitous footpaths, Jake perched precariously on the back of Hezza's Boardman Mountain Pro. Vicky was nowhere to be seen, but Jake seemed to be having a good time – and Tom made a mental note to go round next week for a cup of revolting tea.

* * *

When the bosses from Jesus4All (formerly the Turn or Burn Gospel Coalition) arrived just after lunch, the place was heaving (as were Hezza and Jozee, who had tried to down a quart of milk and then go on the bouncy castle).

Tom spotted the three men walking strangely in step with one another, and moved calmly over to greet them. Harvey walked at their helm, deep-set eyes piously absorbing the jovial scenes at the end of a crow-like nose. The other two members of the trinity stood on either side of the head overseer, all three of them dressed in what the Dulux Colour Chart would have classed as "sanctimonious grey".

"Good afternoon, Harvey, Edward, Oswald."

"Ah, Thomas, good afternoon."

"As you can see, things are really kicking off here."

"Yes, well, it does seem to be the case," Harvey said as he looked around at the satisfied customers, his head swivelling from side to side. "And we are all looking forward to hearing your Gospel exposition later on. Isn't that right, gentlemen?"

Edward and Oswald nodded. Tom noticed that Edward had what must surely be the largest conceivable Adam's apple. It looked as if he'd saved one of Dazza's penalties by swallowing it.

"Would you like a croissant?" Tom offered. Harvey licked his flaking lips.

"Oh, lovely. So, Thomas, when are you going to be preaching to the masses?"

"To be honest, Harvey, I'm not. Dazza – he's the guy getting baptised – has invited a few of the lads from our football team, but we're going to wait until after the crowds have left. It's already a big enough thing for Dazza as it is, without trying to turn him or me into Billy Graham. That's not what we want."

"Yes, I see. Well, you have to make your own choices, Thomas."

"Thanks, Harvey. I think this is best. It's still a remarkable salvation story, though," Tom chuckled.

"Indeed, quite something. Well, we shall see you anon. Is there a lavatory in the vicinity?"

"Yes, over by the weightlifting demonstration. Enjoy the day, and I'll see you later."

Tom was so busy keeping punters feeling welcome and workers full of pastry that he had little chance to chat to everyone he knew. He didn't speak to Kathy all day, but he saw her chatting to Brian the Baptist and the Revd Philip Gallowstree (the meringue-haired, ripple-faced beanpole) as she left, and he wondered what on earth she must think of their theological jousting. She spotted him from across the park and waved a toffee apple. Tom waved a maple and pecan plait, which disintegrated.

* * *

The crowds swelled, thinned and dispersed, and by late afternoon most families had gone home, happy and full, their appetite for fun sated, leaving a few stragglers to squeeze out the last of the thrills.

Amy, having exhausted herself telling anyone who would listen that her daddy owned this park, skipped over to Tom holding a psychedelic lollipop the size of her head. Tom was leaning against a tree, watching Jake throw balls at a coconut.

"Hello, Daddy!"

"Hello, down there. Have you had fun today?"

"Yes, it was very fun… Is that the boy you keep going to see, Daddy?"

"It is indeed, my love. His name is Jake."

"He looks happy."

"Yes. You know, I think he might be."

"But was he sad?"

"Yes, he was sad."

"Why was he sad, Daddy?"

"Well, he was sad because his daddy left home, and he doesn't know when he will see him again."

"Is his daddy at work?"

"Jake doesn't know where his daddy is. That's what makes him sad."

Amy looked across at Tom and took a long, contemplative lick of her lolly.

"Is that how you felt when your daddy left home?"

"…?"

Tom kept his eyes on Jake and coughed twice to get the lump back down his throat.

I didn't even know that she knew.

"Did Mummy tell you that?"

"Yes, Daddy. Mummy said you didn't know where your daddy was and sometimes you felt sad and sometimes you wake up in the night with bad dreams because of your daddy."

The dreams.

"Yes. Yes, that's all true. Yes, my daddy left when I was just a bit younger than Jake, and I felt sad and I didn't know what to do, and I thought it was my fault."

"Mummy's daddy is called Grandad Smiley," Amy said, her tongue now a garish shade of green.

"That's correct."

"Can we go on the bouncy castle now, Daddy?"

"Of course we can."

Amy took Tom by the hand and dragged him over to where a few happy Brutonians were shoelessly jumping to new heights of revelry.

Tom's daughter was still young enough for bouncy inflatables to take precedence over everything else in life. And she was still perhaps too young to hear how Tom's father, an alcoholic naval officer, had shipped out one day and never come home. She was too young to hear how Tom had never understood why; how the anxiety dreams had plagued him ever since; how, for the last three decades, wherever he had been and whatever he had been doing, Tom Hillingthwaite was just a little boy waiting for his daddy to come home.

With his little girl at his side, he took off his shoes and socks, climbed onto the bouncy castle, and jumped himself happier.

* * *

Dazza's baptism was as weird and wonderful as Tom could have expected. As the sun set over Bruton, a small band of well-wishers, including Bill the Boss and about half the Cossacks team, gathered round the dunk tank for the makeshift ceremony. Tom, wearing swimming trunks that brought to mind slaughtered poultry, sat next to Dazza on the spring-release plastic seat and told everyone what it meant to be baptised. Dazza then explained to the throng, haltingly and inarticulately, why Jesus was "O Captain, my Captain". There was some playful jeering, and chants of "What a load of rubbish" from the Revd Gallowstree, after which Bill the Boss kicked a ball at the target mechanism. Both Dazza and Tom plunged into the icy water and came up laughing and shivering. They wrapped themselves in beach towels, embraced in saturated brotherhood, and then Dazza went off to the Lamb and Flag pub to eat, drink and be merry with his comrades.

"Fancy joining us, geezer?" Dazza asked.

"I'm not really into pubs, Dazza. Plus I've got some clearing up to do, so I can't go and get tickled pink. Sorry. But thank you."

"No worries. See ya at the gym. Keep up the good work, yeah?"

"I will."

As Dazza jogged off, Harvey and the other two benefactors from Jesus4All walked in line towards their Community Builder for Wessex.

"Hi, gents. Dazza was just telling me there to keep up the good work."

"Yes, now look, that's all very well, but we're ceasing your contract with immediate effect."

"And I really think that… sorry?"

"You're fired," said Oswald.

"Fired?"

"You heard correctly," Harvey nodded solemnly.

"But I don't…I don't understand. How can you fire me after what you've seen today?"

The three men all gave the same simpering grimace.

"Because," Harvey spoke for them, "the fruits – or should I say fruit – of your entire labour is one single man: a man, to boot, who swore during his testimony and has now gone off to get drunk."

"He became a Christian. What more do you want?"

"He became a Christian, yes. But what about the others? To be fair, Thomas – we do want to be fair, you know – you drew a lot of people to this event. But then you blatantly – spitefully, one might say – refused to share the Gospel with them."

Tom's pupils dilated. The tips of his fingers were tingling.

"But…"

"But it's not just that, is it? No." Harvey swivelled his head towards the man on his left. "Edward, would you please pass me that letter? We received this missive from a Penelope Quinn, whom I think you know?"

Tom's head was ringing, his heart not so much sinking as plummeting.

"She says here in this letter that you've been acting inappropriately towards a young lad at the school."

"Inappropriately? That's rubbish! Harvey, that's utter rubbish! Mrs Quinn just thinks that I've been Bible-bashing Jake, the young lad I've been mentoring – but I haven't. I haven't. I was given strict orders to avoid too much autobiography. I never once even spoke about God."

"Then why is she saying these things? There's no smoke without fire. Also, what was the point of you being there, if not to actually share the Gospel? This all seems symptomatic of a wider trend, you see."

"Wha…" Tom's voice tailed off. The eyes beneath Harvey's jutting brow showed by their implacability that this wasn't a fair hearing. It was a sentencing.

"Do you have anything to say, Thomas?"

Tom looked at Harvey, then at the glistening dunk tank, and considered editing his prayer about no drownings.

"Do I have anything to say? Lots. But to you three? Nothing."

"Very well. We will pay you until the end of next month, but please be out of your house by the first."

"But that's next Friday – that's less than a week."

"Yes, not ideal, I know, but we want to have the new chap moving in as soon as possible – we're bringing down our man from Mercia. We shall, of course, pay for the removal van."

"…?"

"Every good wish, then."

Harvey, Edward and Oswald turned as one and walked away, taking Tom's career with them.

Tom realised that he had probably been a dead man walking long before Harvey and his co-sponsors had made the drive down to Bruton. He could have baptised the entire Lamb and Flag Cossacks team today, and the result would have been the same; the writing was already graffitied onto the wall. Through a mind clogged with numbness, one thought struggled out.

This isn't just about salvations. This is about control.

Tom had faced many difficulties since moving to Wessex but, throughout, his overbearing bosses had been his real bane. And now they had broken his back.

Chapter 19

Parson's Farewell

A week passed quickly. By Friday morning, the damp-infested house was once more full of boxes – sealed, stacked and in the process of being loaded onto a van by two miscellaneous removal henchmen.

The job of packing up had been made much easier for the Hillingthwaites by the presence of the people of Dews Close. To a man, they gave up time that week to help their neighbours prepare for the move.

"Can't 'ave a pregnant lady lifting boxes all on 'er own, can we?" said Wayne the Tattooligan, single-handedly lugging the leather lazy-boy from the man-cave.

"Shouldn't you be doing this, lazy boy?" he asked Tom.

"It needs a real man," Tom replied placatingly. The human collage offered Tom a big, broad, cavernous grin from his five-a-side goal-mouth.

I won't miss that.

As they locked up the house for the final time, Catrina and Not-Carl walked round with a big see-through Tupperware packed with sandwiches.

"This should keep you fed until you get over the border,"

Catrina said with a smile. "There's bacon in yours, Tom."

Tom was moved.

"Thanks, guys. Thank you, Catrina and… I'm sorry, I don't know your name."

Not-Carl looked obliquely at the man who had lived two doors down for the last six months.

"It's Tom. My name's Tom."

"Oh, the same as mine. That should be easy to remember, then."

Not-Carl/Tom shook his head confoundedly, then shook his namesake's hand and went off to work on his rockery.

The Kung-Fu Gardener had prepared a special leaving ceremony for Tom and his family, in which he put a can of pop on top of a wheelie bin and then kicked it off into the bushes.

"Steven Segal!" he cried, his hands raised worshipfully to the sky.

"I'm sure the new man from the ministry will enjoy living here," Tom said to Anne as the old lady loaded a spaciously caged Selina into the car.

"Yes, we are quite the community these days. I just hope he doesn't try to wash my car, that's all. Have a safe trip."

With all the family seated in the car, the inhabitants of Dews Close waved goodbye to the Hillingthwaite family for the last time. Tom put the red Sedan into gear and rolled out of the cul-de-sac and onto the main road, throwing his last remaining business card out of the window as he did so. They would head north to Scotland, to stay with Rachel's parents until Tom could find more work. But first, Tom had one final visit to make. His abrupt sacking had killed dead so many half-finished projects – and most of them would have to stay where they lay. But there was one person Tom needed to see before he left. One relationship that would not have the life kicked out of it.

* * *

Tom parked the car outside Roundhouse Primary School and got out.

"Back in a minute," he said, squeezing Rachel's hand.

"Am I going to school now, Daddy?"

"No, you're not. I am. Daddy just has one more lesson…"

Tom no longer had the requisite clearance to enter Roundhouse Primary School – it had been revoked along with all his other passes and memberships. But he still held one pass that couldn't be rescinded or laminated, and she was named Kathy.

She met him at the door, a look of measured authority on her face. She still held some power at Roundhouse, and she was using it now without impunity.

"Don't be too long," she said.

"Thanks, Kathy."

"It really is my pleasure, Tom. Oh, and I went to Brian's church on Sunday. It was a bit weird to be back somewhere like that, but… well, we'll see."

"We will indeed," Tom nodded with a knowing grin. "Just make sure that when you go back next time, you take your own flipping biscuits with you."

The headmistress's power-guise burst and a bark of a laugh shot around the lobby. Instantly regaining her dignity, she covered her mouth with her hand and shooed Tom away. The shooing turned into a wave, which turned into a bow. Then Kathy went back to her office, and got on with the business of the day.

Tom's plap-plapping feet entered the Memorial Hall. It was empty, save for one person – the one person Tom had hoped not to see.

Petefeast Clark was laying out mats for the lunchtime martial arts club he ran. His body freeze-framed as soon as he saw Tom. Tom tensed too, and was about to say something conciliatory when Petefeast suddenly smiled.

"Oh, hi, Tom. I didn't expect to see you again."

Eh?

This was the first thing Petefeast had ever said to him that wasn't either mocking or combative.

"Hi there, Pete."

Petefeast padded over to where Tom was standing like a hedgehog facing down a juggernaut.

"Look," he said, "I know we weren't the best of friends during your time here, but I just wanted to shake your hand and say 'no hard feelings'. I wish you all the best."

Tom couldn't believe what he was hearing. Petefeast had threatened to make him pay for breaking up his fling with Kathy, but there was no threat in his voice, and Petefeast's hands were spread wide, palms open. Why the dramatic change of tone?

Has Dazza had a word with him at the gym?

With a confused but relieved smile, Tom reached out and took the proffered hand. Pete smiled again – an odd smile, which Tom realised too late was totally detached from the eyes.

The fist that slammed into Tom's gut was like a bolt from the blue. Flinching and crumpling, Tom's knees hit the karate mat hard, his body kept upright by Pete's amicable handshake.

"Get up," Pete said breezily. Without waiting for a reply, he pulled Tom to his feet and hit him even harder – a precision punch where no bruise would show. Tom felt the wind leave his body in a hurry. His insides felt instantly vacuum-packed.

"It's fine, mate, it's fine, it happens – it's life." Pete's soothing tones were chilling. This was not the first time he had exacted vengeance on a foe; he had no regret, no issue. He un-manacled Tom's hand and watched his victim drop helplessly to the mat. Petefeast Clark rubbed his palms together in a hand-washing fashion, then padded casually out of the hall without a backward glance.

Tom remained kneeling on the mat, mewing and retching as he watched a string of saliva navigate its way to the floor. There was no air – just pain. He wanted to cry, to scream, to hit Petefeast back. But he didn't. He couldn't.

Get up.

"No."

Get up.

"No, I can't."

Get up, Thomas.

He got up. Tom Hillingthwaite got up. Gripping his stomach, his throat threatening to open like a sluice gate for a river of vomit, he stood up – and started walking. The sound of his plimsolls padding along the corridor had never seemed more pathetic, but the sound of his soul crying out in agony and defiance was the only thing Tom chose to hear.

The population of Yellow Set was sitting on his "thinking chair" outside Mrs Quinn's classroom. He had heard Tom coming: he would have known that plap-plap-plapping anywhere.

"Hi, Jake."

"Hi."

"'Thinking chair' again? What was it this time?"

"Punched another boy."

Another storming Hillingthwaite success.

"Argh, Jake, you know it's not…"

"He said you was stupid, so I hit him."

"Eh?"

"Ryan said it was good you was leaving 'cos you're dead stupid, so I hit him in his horrible face."

"Oh. Right. Well, I mean, thank y– I mean, you still shouldn't have… OK."

From his "thinking chair", Jake looked up at Tom and asked the question he had obviously been thinking about since Mrs Quinn had cheerfully broken the news about Tom's sacking.

"When will you come back?"

That was it. That was the question: the question Jake had been asking ever since he woke up one morning and found his dad was gone. It was the same question Tom had been asking for three decades, and suddenly Tom saw himself at eight years of age sitting not in a corridor, but in the back seat of his mum's car, asking, "When will Daddy come back?"

But his mum didn't answer. She just sat in silence.

That silence had haunted Tom throughout the last thirty years, and now it spanned the decades to grab him by the throat.

Tom had been a professional. From the first time he met Jake, he had wanted to say so much. To make it better. But he had remained silent.

No religion, no autobiography.

He wouldn't allow silence to have the final word here, though. He wouldn't let another little boy go through life without an answer to that horrible question.

Tom dropped to his knees, meeting Jake at eye-level.

"Jake, I can't tell you when I'll come back. I don't even know that I will come back."

Jake's jaw clenched noticeably tighter. His fingers were tapping out the beat of his heart on his hand-me-down trousers. Tom's insides were groaning with pain, both physical and everything else.

"But Jake, I want you to know that I'm not leaving because of you. And I want you to know… I want you to know that my dad left, too. I was a bit younger than you – I don't even remember what he looked like apart from photos – but it broke my heart and I didn't know what to do. And nobody understood what it was like, even if they said they did."

Tom's throat was so tight and his eyes were leaking. As he continued, he wasn't even sure which little boy he was addressing any more.

"I want you to know that Dad didn't leave because of you. He didn't leave because of you. I still don't know why he left, but it wasn't my– it wasn't because of you. You're not a stupid little boy."

Jake gave a curt nod.

"Tell me that you know that, Jake. Tell me that you know it wasn't because of you."

"…"

"Jake?"

Jake didn't speak. But he slowly, very slowly, started to cry. The pent-up fear and rage and distress and despair that he had kept locked away and hidden in his internal boy-cave came out now. The mask came off and darkness fell from behind it. Throwing himself from his chair, Jake buried his face in Tom's battered midriff and Tom held him. And held him. And held him.

And Jake wept. And he wept and he wept.

And Tom Hillingthwaite wept too. Through his tears he insisted, "Tell me you know it wasn't because of you. I need to hear you say it."

"I know," came a still small voice from Tom's abdomen. "I know it wasn't because of me."

"Good, Jake. That's so good. Please, always remember that. Always remember that, because there are times when you need to tell yourself that. I'm proud of you for saying that."

Tom unbuckled Jake from his own body and placed him at arm's length, his hands on the boy's shoulders.

"And there's one more thing, Jake. The most important thing. There is a Father who loves you. There is. And he's not going anywhere. He loves you more than anything."

Tom unzipped his jacket and pulled out a familiar face.

"I want you to have this. I've been calling him Barney, but really his name's Little Tom. He's really good to talk to when you're feeling low."

Jake took the puppet in his hands and held it to his stomach.

A pair of eyes suddenly appeared at the classroom window. Mrs Quinn was staring hard, alerted by the sound of crying from the corridor.

The door swung open and there she was, looking down at Tom with unmitigated distaste.

"What are you two talking about, then?" she said through unmoving teeth.

"Oh, Mrs Quinn, I'm glad you're here. I was just telling Jake that God loves him."

"I beg your pardon? You are not permitted to do that, Mr Hillingthwaite –you're not even allowed to be here."

Tom rose to his feet, looked Mrs Quinn squarely in the face, and licked his lips.

"Deal with it," he said. "Deal. With. It."

And with that, Tom gave her his biggest, broadest smile, doffed an imaginary cap to Jake, and plip-plapped out of Roundhouse Primary School for the final time, his body crashing, his soul soaring.

* * *

Tom got into the car and started the engine.

"You OK?" Rachel asked.

"Yes, thanks," Tom said. "I was just passing on the cowl."

"I have no idea what that means, honeybunny."

"You don't need to, my chosen."

Tom looked at the sun visor to which he had attached two pictures – one of Jesus (played by Jim Caviezel), and one of his

233

unborn child's twelve-week scan. They were there to remind Tom that firstly, someone died for him, and secondly, that nobody in the world was more blessed.

"Let's go, shall we? Everyone ready?"

"Are we going north, Daddy?" Amy asked from the back seat.

"Yes, my love. North."

And upwards.

Epilogue

The knocking on the door of No. 3 Dews Close went unanswered. The doorbell rang out, but there was no sound from within. He tried the gate to the garden, but it was locked and bolted.

The land line had been disconnected, too. He knew he had the right number; he had rung it so many times, but when it was answered he had never quite plucked up the courage to say "Hello". Now, though, when the courage was there, nobody was at home.

The man with the broken nose and salt-and-pepper beard looked anxiously around.

"Can I help you?" asked an elderly woman next door, who had come outside to tend her roses.

"Thomas Hillingthwaite," said the man.

"Oh, they don't live here any more, I'm afraid. They've gone to Scotland, to her parents."

"I see. Thank you."

The man stepped down from the front door and walked back towards the main road. Lying on the path in the cul-de-sac was a business card. He picked it up and stared curiously at the name on it. The lady tending her roses called after him.

"Are you all right? Is there anything I can help with?"

"No, no, really. Thank you."

How do I get to Scotland?

The man looked again at the name on the card.

"Tom Hillingthwaite".

It was a familiar name. And a good one.

It was the name that, thirty-seven years earlier, the man with the broken nose and salt-and-pepper beard had given to his son.

A Spot of Housekeeping

*H*uge thanks must go to Tony Collins and all the staff at Monarch, for once again giving me the chance to publish. This book has been a while in the making and Tony has exhibited great forbearance, but I suppose a publisher learns to have forbearance shortly after he learns to spell it.

Thanks also to Becca, for exhibiting so much grace in doing all the childcare while I locked myself away to write. The date nights are on me, Wifey!

And to my agent, Greg, who has kept the gigs coming at just the right pace during the brain-melting editing phase. To book a comedy- or book-related event, get in touch with Greg via www.thecomedyagency.co.uk.

And finally, to Dee Williamson, my Writing Director. For all the mentoring and honing and shouting and exemplifying. And the laughing. There is no Tom without you, so thanks.

Now then…

As with all my books, there are pop-culture references, song lyrics and lines from films buried in the text. You can get in touch and let me know which ones you've found if you like – it makes the writing of the thing more fun that way.

As I write this, I don't know where Tom will end up – whether the Hillingthwaites will settle in Scotland or move on quickly. I do know that there is another story to tell, and I hope to tell it at some point.

Tom Hillingthwaite will suretainly return.

Andy
#SGCS
andy@andykind.co.uk
@andykindcomedy on Twitter
www.andykind.co.uk